OUTLAWS' LOOT

OUTLAWS' LOOT

by

Mark Falcon

Dales Large Print Books
Long Preston, North Yorkshire,
BD23 4ND, England.

1862623532

CO13633082

British Library Cataloguing in Publication Data.

Falcon, Mark
    Outlaws' loot.

    A catalogue record of this book is
    available from the British Library

    ISBN   1-84262-353-2 pbk

First published in Great Britain 2004 by Robert Hale Limited

Copyright © Mark Falcon 2004

Cover illustration © Longaron by arrangement with
Norma Editorial Ltd.

Published in Large Print 2005 by arrangement with
Robert Hale Ltd.

Dales Large Print is an imprint of Library Magna Books Ltd.

Printed and bound in Great Britain by
T.J. (International) Ltd., Cornwall, PL28 8RW

To Margaret Pickering

CHAPTER ONE

It was always a sad time for the cowboys after the round-up was over and the selected stock was driven to the market. The work was hard with long hours in the saddle, either eating dust or crouching low so the rain did not penetrate their slickers, but somehow it always did.

Most of the men were discharged after their job was done and they drifted around looking for work to keep them going throughout the winter. Some were lucky and were kept on to do tasks about the ranch such as fence-mending, or even living out the winter in the line camps where they would keep an eye on the remnants of the herd, which would be the nucleus for the next generation.

Jesse Cahill was the oldest of the four who were packing their gear in the bunkhouse, ready for an unknown destination. The other ten men had already said their goodbyes and left. They had become firm friends over the past year, although when Jesse thought about it, none of them knew that much about the others, mostly only their first names or names that had been given to them by others, such as the place they had been brought up in – Kentucky Pete, Abilene Joe, Texas Bill, usually abbreviated to Kentucky, Abilene or Texas.

'Have we decided which way we're headin'?' Johnny Diamond asked the older man, whom the three tended to look to for leadership.

'Waal, I've bin thinkin',' Jesse answered in his usual, slow drawl. He was a broad-shouldered man, six feet four in height, and forty-three years old. He opened up one of his saddle-bags and produced a newspaper which was now about four months old.

'I was gonna use this for other purposes,' his blue eyes twinkled in a smile, 'but I found it kinda interesting. It's an article about the Bassett gang and how they were all caught because a young girl escaped from their hideout and gave the whereabouts of the place to the law. I feel kinda sorry for her, as it says here,' he tapped the paper with a large hand, 'that in spite of her informing on the gang to the law, she was given a ten-year prison sentence for riding with them on a bank raid. Others did verify that she was forced into it by her stepfather and Hay Bassett, but the judge seemed to have taken a disliking to the girl and gave her ten years.'

Jesse's words interested the three men immediately.

'So the whole gang are now in prison?' the sandy-haired, twenty-eight-year-old Joel McRory asked.

'No, they're all dead, including the girl. Most of them died in a fire at one of their hideouts called Larkinton. The law set light to the town when they wouldn't surrender. It seems that the girl was up in the hills with the leader, Hay Bassett, who had taken her for his woman. The posse rescued her after Bassett shot the girl's stepfather, Denver Branch, who was about to kill her.'

'Wow!' Johnny Diamond exclaimed. 'But I thought you said the girl died too.'

'Yeah. She was being transported to the next town to serve her prison sentence together with two other prisoners. Let's see now.' Jesse opened the pages to refresh his memory. 'Here it is. One was Jim Tobin and the other was a man called Hankins. He used to work for her stepfather before they joined up with the Bassett gang. It says here that Hankins somehow got away before the wagon went over a ravine. A US marshal who was following them killed Hankins in a shoot-out.'

'What's all this leading to?' Joel asked as he finished packing up his blanket roll with his slicker on the outside.

'Just think fer a minute,' said Jesse. 'The Bassett gang had been operating since after the war without being caught as no one knew where their hideout was. Not until this girl informed on them.'

'So?' Johnny Diamond encouraged.

'So, my friends, I'd like to know what happened to all the money they stole over the years.'

The three looked thoughtful for a minute until Joel said:

'Mebbe it all got burnt in the fire in that place called Larkinton.'

Jesse nodded, then added, 'But that other hideout – Paradise as it was called – didn't get burned. What happened to Hay Bassett's loot?'

As yet the youngest of the trio facing Jesse had not spoken. No one was surprised at this as the equally tall, fair-haired young man hardly ever spoke. The others often made fun of him but nothing seemed to rile the man. He just smiled and took it all good-humouredly.

'What do you think, Jude?' Jesse asked the twenty-five-year-old.

Jude shrugged his shoulders. 'Mebbe the money's still there somewhere – unless someone else has found it.'

'What say we go and take a look around?' Jesse suggested. 'We could mebbe stay in the cabin that's up there for the winter.'

'Waal, we've gotta find somewhere to stay until the spring round-up,' said Johnny Diamond, 'It might as well be there – unless of course the place is already occupied.'

'How do we find this "Paradise"?' asked Joel. 'If the law couldn't find it after all these years, how do you expect us to?'

'Because,' Jesse began, 'this girl who gave the Bassett gang away to the law, drew a picture of the shape of the rocks where the entrance is. It's about forty miles south of a town called Hazelworth – that's the same town whose bank the Bassett gang and the girl robbed before she escaped from them.'

'OK,' said Johnny, 'I'm for it.'

'Yeah, me too,' Joel added.

The three looked at Jude, who nodded his agreement to the plan.

Jesse led the way through the door of the bunkhouse without a backward glance. They had been paid off and the money had

13

to last them until they signed on again in the spring. Their horses were soon saddled and the four set off in the general direction of Hazelworth, Colorado, about fifty miles away, from where they would get their bearings and set off on the last lap of their journey to Paradise.

CHAPTER TWO

The cabin door and window faced east and the early morning sun streamed through the window. The light from it made it possible for Steve Culley to see the sleeping girl by his side. He looked down at her beautiful face, surrounded by a mass of flame-coloured hair.

He still could not believe she was finally his. It was about five months since he'd first met her, when he and his partner were tracking mavericks on one side of the river that separated the Johnson spread, where they worked, from the Big B Ranch, where Kelly lived with her stepfather and mother. She was lying on her back in the slow-flowing water, minus her clothes, completely unaware of their presence to begin with. He remembered with a smile how flustered and embarrassed she was when she realized she was being watched.

They had met at the same place several times after that. The first time it seemed as if it had been a coincidence, but after that the meetings were prearranged.

Steve also remembered the last time he had seen her at that spot, when Denver Branch her stepfather and his two men had come upon them while Steve and Kelly had kissed for the first time. That was the moment that she had fallen in love with him. He was already in love with her from the first time they met.

Such a lot had happened since that day she was dragged off and Steve had been badly beaten by Denver Branch's two men. Kelly had been forced to go with her stepfather and his men with the Bassett gang, who had called at their place. It was three months later when Steve met her again, here in this place the Bassett gang called Paradise. He remembered how bad he had felt when Kelly had told him Hay Bassett, his own father, had already made love to her. During her time with the outlaws, she had become fond of the man and he had protected her from

15

his men, and Kelly was sure she would never see Steve again. He was not sure he could accept this at the time, but Kelly had assured Steve that she had always loved him and always would. Later when he had gone after the prison wagon after she had been given a ten year sentence, he had found that she was nearly three months pregnant with Hay Bassett's child.

It had been thirteen years since Steve had last seen his father, when Hay Bassett had left him and his mother for the last time. Unknown to Bassett, he had left his wife pregnant, and it had been Steve who had helped deliver his brother when he himself was only twelve years old. His mother had remarried later and Steve had taken his new stepfather's name of Culley.

Kelly stirred beside him and opened her eyes and looked up into Steve's grey eyes looking down at her. His heartbeats quickened at the beautiful smile she gave him.

'The sun's up, it must be getting late,' she said, moving to get out of bed.

Steve pulled her down again. 'No need to get up yet. We've got all day.'

Kelly laughed. 'We'll get lazy if we don't make a start.'

'In a minute,' Steve said and kissed her

firmly on the lips. How he wished she had belonged fully to him first, instead of his father, Hay Bassett. Then there was Jim Tobin, to whom she was shackled in the prison wagon, together with Hankins, one of the men who had beat him up so badly. If only Hankins hadn't bushwhacked him one night when Steve was following the trio after they had escaped from the guards. The bullet had creased his skull and he had lost his memory for a while. He had even forgotten Kelly and rejected her. That was why she had ridden off with Jim Tobin and the two had become lovers.

'I love you, Steve,' Kelly whispered as his kisses became more urgent.

But she had loved Tobin on the trail and the two had returned to Paradise to live together here in the cabin. If Steve had not been here before them, Tobin would not have wanted a showdown. The man would always believe that Kelly had Steve on her mind. Only one of them could have her and he had forced Steve to have a final shoot-out to settle things once and for all. The outcome was that Steve was kissing her at that moment.

He pulled away from her and lay beside her. Kelly was four months with child and he knew he would have to wait until after the baby was born before they could become as one.

'You do still love me, Steve, don't you – in spite of everything?' It was as if she had been reading his mind.

'You needn't doubt it,' he replied. 'I'll get the stove going.' He walked over to the centre of the large room in his longjohns and started a fire in the stove using some hay under the firewood as kindling.

While he was doing this Kelly got dressed. Satisfied that the fire was going well, Steve got dressed himself and went outside to fetch water from the stream.

It was the last week in September and the weather was still warm but Steve knew it could change at any time now.

'I'd better take the wagon and get supplies before winter sets in, Kelly,' he said, filling the coffee pot from the pail.

'I suppose so,' said Kelly. 'Shall I come with you?'

'Mebbe you'd better stay here. I won't be able to go to Hazelworth, which is closer, so I'll have to go in the other direction to another town. It'll be a bumpy ride and I reckon it'll take two days there and two back.'

Kelly nodded. 'I won't like being here on my own. I can't bear the thought of not seeing you for four whole days!'

Steve gave a short laugh. 'We've got the rest of our lives together, Kelly.'

She nodded. 'All the same...'

'I'll go after breakfast. The sooner I go, the sooner I'll be home.' He reassured her with a kiss.

Kelly packed up some food for his journey, and gave him two full canteens of water. As they said their goodbyes at the two boulders by the track, Kelly felt very uneasy at being left alone – the first time she had ever been alone in her life.

'You will come back to me, won't you, Steve?'

Steve frowned. 'Why on earth wouldn't I? I might have been a fool once and let you go off with Jim Tobin, but I came to my senses after you'd left and I'll never lose them again. Of course I'll come back to you. It would take my death for me not to.'

Kelly felt a cold shiver run down her back at his last words. She knew she was being stupid thinking the worst, but something didn't feel quite right.

Steve hitched up the horses to the wagon on the other side of the narrow path and jumped aboard. They waved to each other and Kelly watched as the wagon disappeared round a bend in the roadway.

Kelly knew she ought to make use of the time making baby clothes or even clothes for herself. She had only the one dress which she was wearing, bought for her by Jim Tobin in one of the towns she had stopped at with him and Hankins while eluding the law. She swallowed hard at the memory of Jim. She had loved him while they were together, as she thought she would never see Steve again. She had since realized that she would never have allowed herself to have such feelings for the man if she had known that she and Steve would meet up once more.

There would not be many more warm days left before winter, Kelly realized, and she decided to make the most of it by having a swim in the pool down in the valley.

Jesse Cahill and his three companions made a stopover in Hazelworth. They indulged themselves with a bed each at the hotel and a hot bath and shave. It felt good becoming a clean human being again after roughing it during the round-up. They were well aware, however, that they would have to watch how they spent their money as it had to last them until the spring when the season started all over again.

Jesse and the others paid the town's saloon a visit and were soon laughing and joking over a few beers. One of the saloon girls sashayed towards the four as they sat round a table. It was difficult to tell her age under all that heavy make-up, but Jesse figured her to be older than she was trying look. He felt a little sorry for her, in fact he felt sorry for all the women who needed to make a living the way she did. There was not much work around for single women. If they hadn't got a man to support them then they had to do something to stay alive.

'Wanna buy me a drink, boys?' She smiled down at them.

Jesse tossed a dollar over to her on the table. She picked it up and put it between her ample bosoms.

'Thanks, mister. Anything I can do for you?' she asked and looked up at the balcony with three doors beyond.

Jesse shook his head, but Joel was quick to realize what she was offering. He drank down the last of his beer and took her by the hand, smiling at his three companions before he was led away up the stairs.

'She was about your age, Jesse,' Johnny Diamond remarked. 'I shoulda thought you'd like a bit of female company after looking at steers' backsides for months.'

Jesse just smiled and stood up with his empty glass in his hand.

'One more before I turn in for the night, I reckon. How about you two?'

They both nodded and Jesse fetched three more beers.

By the time they had finished their drinks Joel had still not returned.

'He's making a night of it, I reckon.' Johnny grinned. 'He'll be paying for two beds tonight, the fool, and his will stay empty.'

The three cowboys headed for the batwing doors. A chill wind blew outside.

'It won't be long before winter sets in,' Jesse remarked. 'I hope that cabin is vacant when we get there. It'll be a long ride for nothing if it's already occupied.'

'Do you reckon we ought to buy supplies tomorrow before we leave?' Jude asked. The other two were surprised he had spoken.

'It might be as well.' Jesse nodded. 'We'll need to eat wherever we make camp for the winter.'

'Maybe we could get work here for a while?' Johnny Diamond suggested. 'Our pay won't hold out too long.'

'You can try it if you want,' Jesse replied. 'I'm going on to that place called Paradise. Who knows, if we find the Bassett gang's loot, we can buy a spread of our own and never have to work for anyone else again.'

'It sounds like a good idea,' said Johnny, tossing back his long dark hair. 'But if we don't find it, things could be tough for us – me in particular.' Things had been harder for the half-breed than the others. Not many ranchers would take on Indians, Mexicans or blacks. If they did, they earned far less than the other cow waddies, which itself was not all that much. The maximum a waddie could earn was fifty dollars a month. Younger, inexperienced hands and non-whites only got twenty-five to thirty dollars. Jesse's money was more as he was also a 'bronc peeler' and earned five dollars for each bronc he 'busted', and would typically work around six to eight horses a day. Jesse was under no illusions about how long this extra string to his bow would last. It only needed just one particular 'sunfisher' to throw him awkwardly and he could break his bones and be laid up for months, possibly for ever. He was no longer young, either; it could happen at any time. He had seen several former 'peelers' reduced to becoming a chuck wagon cook.

Johnny knew he was worth more than he was paid but there was nothing much he could do about it. He was neither white nor Indian and the man would always have a chip on his shoulder. He had ridden with Jesse and the other three for two years now and they all treated him as their equal, which he knew he was. He resolved he would go with the others to Paradise, no matter how things turned out, good or bad.

CHAPTER THREE

Joel awoke the next morning with a man inside his head hammering to get out – or so it seemed. What the devil had happened to him the night before? he asked himself. He didn't remember drinking too excessively.

There was a movement beside him in the bed and he suddenly realized where he was. The woman turned over and started snoring loudly. Joel took this to mean it was time he was leaving. He still had his socks and longjohns on and he pulled on his pants and buttoned up his shirt.

He decided not to wake the sleeping beauty and closed the door quietly behind him.

The barkeep was sweeping soiled sawdust into a heap in a corner when he descended the stairs to the saloon. There were spots of blood among it, Joel noticed, and he reckoned he'd missed out on a fight in the saloon after he'd left his companions. He only hoped the fight didn't include Jesse and the others, although he knew they could well take care of themselves.

Joel walked down the street and entered the hotel. He noticed Jesse, Jude and Johnny about to descend the stairs.

'Did you have a good night?' Johnny grinned as he led the way down to the hotel foyer.

'Huh!' Joel grunted. 'I wish the hell I knew! I remember handing over ten dollars and she gave me a drink – wine she called it. After tossing it down I can't remember a goddam thing. I reckon she drugged me or something.'

'Waal, she is getting on in years for that kind of work. Mebbe she wanted a good night's sleep,' Jesse suggested with a twinkle in his blue eyes.

'But I paid her ten dollars!' Joel exclaimed. 'I have to work a week for that! I've a good mind to go back for a refund – or a free one.'

'Put it down to experience.' Jesse smiled.

Joel slouched out of the hotel, shoulders hunched and thumbs in the pockets of his Levis.

'Waal, I've a good mind to go back to the hotel and get a refund on the room. I never used it!'

'I've a feelin' the proprietor wouldn't take too kindly to that suggestion,' said Jesse, slapping his friend on the back. 'A lesson learned is a lesson earned.'

Joel growled. 'I need some coffee. My head's thumping like a war drum.'

The four made their way to the restaurant down the street a way and ordered some breakfast to go with the coffee.

An hour later the men were loading supplies on to their horses, evening out the load between them, and were soon on their way towards their intended winter camp in the mountains.

One night was spent on the trail and then they were off again. Towards noon Jesse produced the newspaper report that had set them off on their quest for the outlaws' loot.

The shape of the mountains which the girl had originally drawn on a scrap of paper that an old prospector had provided when she had met him whilst escaping from the gang, was reproduced in the newspaper cutting now in Jesse's hands. They had not come to the spot yet and Jesse wondered if they could have missed it.

About a mile further on the familiar shapes of the mountains came into view.

'There it is!' Jesse exclaimed in excitement. 'Come on, boys, we're almost there!'

Jesse's tone encouraged the three to urge their mounts forward at a faster pace. It might have been a hare-brained scheme of Jesse's, but the thought of actually finding Hay Bassett's hidden loot brightened up their hard lives.

Within an hour they had reached the entrance to the box canyon that once hid the outlaws' town of Larkinton. As they rode along the narrow pathway, wide enough only for a wagon to pass through, they stopped in unison and looked around at the desolate sight before them. Grass and stunted bushes were beginning to grow through the ashes that were once buildings, mostly made of wood.

'To think,' said Jesse, 'that because of that

girl, this place was razed to the ground.'

'And then she ends up at the bottom of a ravine,' Johnny Diamond added.

'Yeah,' Joel added. 'I'm not sure if I feel sorry for her or not.'

Jesse shrugged his shoulders. 'Depends which side of the law you're on, I reckon. I think she was pretty brave. It couldn't have been much fun for her, being kept a prisoner by a gang of outlaws.'

'You always do feel sorry for people,' Joel told him. 'It'll be your downfall one of these days. Someone'll take advantage of your kind heart.'

They had continued on their course by now and after a while they came to the narrow ledge which led to the cabin.

Johnny Diamond drew in his breath and whistled.

'This ain't exactly a track you'd want to use regular.'

'What's wrong, Johnny – scared?' Joel goaded.

'We've every right to be careful,' Jesse pointed out. 'But if that girl could ride over here, then so can we. Keep tight against the side of the mountain. Your mount's only got to stumble and...' Jesse left the sentence unfinished.

'I'll go first.'

The mouths of the three opened simultaneously in surprise at Jude Cameron's words. Not only had he spoken for the first time that day, but he was offering to lead them across the dangerous path.

'OK, Jude. Go ahead.' Jesse grinned. There was more to this quiet man than most people realized. Jesse probably knew him best and he respected the young man more than he had ever told him. He knew he could trust and rely on him implicitly as he had found out over the past two years of riding together.

Jude set off slowly but confidently, taking care not to alarm his mount in any way. He was followed by Jesse, then Johnny and Joel.

There were two boulders, one on each side of the track at the other end and once the four had passed between them the cabin came into view.

'There ain't no horses in the corral,' Joel observed. 'I can't see no smoke coming outa the chimney either. Looks like the place is deserted.'

'Yeah,' Jesse agreed, 'but let's not get too confident. There could be a rifle aiming straight at us on the other side of that door.'

'Let's approach it from the left and work

29

our way round from the corral,' said Johnny. 'There's no windows on that side.'

The others nodded and did as Johnny suggested.

They dismounted at the corral and tied their mounts to the fence.

'I'll go in first,' said Jude, which received another set of open mouths.

Jude walked quietly towards the cabin door. It was shut but when he gave it a gentle push with his booted toe, it opened slowly.

'Anyone in there?' Jude called out.

There was no answer.

'We're coming in!' Jude announced.

He pushed the door fully open and peered around the door-frame into the one large room. There was no sound or movement and Joel went in further.

'It's OK, no one at home,' Jude told them.

The three men followed him inside and looked around them. The place was sparsely furnished with a pot-bellied stove in the centre of the room and a long table and a form on each side. It was obvious that this place had once been occupied by several people – the Bassett gang – otherwise there would have been no need for such a long table. There was a tall cupboard at the far end of the room and two chairs, and a double bed in the far corner.

Jesse moved forward and ran his finger over the table and the cupboard.

'Waal, there's no trace of dust. There's a double bed in the corner and the place looks as if it's had a woman's touch. A man on his own wouldn't bother to do any dusting.'

The others grinned and nodded in agreement.

'I reckon you're right, Jesse,' said Joel. 'But where is she?'

'Mebbe her and her man have gone to town for supplies,' was Johnny's suggestion.

'You could well be right, Johnny.' Jesse touched the coffee pot. 'It's slightly warm. Must've bin used this morning. I suggest we get this stove going and boil us a pot of coffee. One of you go and fetch the coffee beans.'

Joel was nearest the door at that moment and went to fetch them.

Kelly had enjoyed her swim. The water was always icy cold, no matter what the weather, but she soon got used to it. After about half an hour of either swimming or lying on her back in the water and looking up at the blue sky, she got out and dried herself. The graves

31

of Hay Bassett and Jim Tobin were a few feet away and she felt as if the two men who had loved her were watching her as she got dressed. She blinked away a tear that had come into her eyes and tried to put them from her mind. But she knew they would always be there at some time in the days ahead.

Kelly began to walk up the gentle slope towards the cabin. It would feel very lonely without Steve. How she wished the next few days would pass quickly and he would return to her.

She had almost reached the stream from where they got their water, which was about ten feet from the cabin. She stopped suddenly and her heart began to race. There were four horses tied to the corral fence!

CHAPTER FOUR

Kelly wondered if anyone had seen her from the window. She felt vulnerable. Her gun, which she had vowed never to use again, was inside the cabin – and so was the legacy given to her by Doc Reynolds. He had been struck off as a doctor and surgeon after the Civil War had ended and the horrors of all he had encountered had made him turn to drink. After he had performed surgery whilst drunk one day the patient had died. Doc Reynolds had been struck off, and Hay Bassett had taken him on as doctor to the gang and also for those other outlaws hiding out in Larkinton. He had tended to Kelly's injuries after the gang had forced her to fight the youngest of the gang, Sandy Kaye, to prove herself. Up to that moment all the gang, except for her stepfather and his two men, Quincey and Hankins, and also Hay Bassett who had gone on ahead to Paradise, were unaware that she was a girl and not the boy she had disguised herself as. Kelly and Jim had ridden nearly as far as the Wyoming border after their flight from the law, and Kelly had met the doctor in a town and agreed to meet him again the same night. She was surprised when Doc Reynolds had handed her a parcel containing twenty thousand dollars, saying that he had not long to live and no one to leave his life savings to. He said Kelly deserved the money after all she had gone through with the gang.

Perhaps the men inside the cabin would not find the money? Kelly sincerely hoped it would be safe in its hiding-place.

She moved quickly to her right and hid herself behind the privy, which was nearly opposite the cabin. She would wait, she decided, and see what happened next. As long as they hadn't seen her, she would be safe. But she knew that she couldn't stay out in the open for too long. She would need food and a drink.

After what seemed hours, but was only one hour, three men came out of the cabin and were making their way towards the valley where Kelly had come from a while earlier. She felt lucky she hadn't lingered by the pool for any longer or she would have been caught.

She wondered who the men could be. She had not seen a lawman's badge on their vests and by the look of their dress she guessed they were cowboys. It occurred to her that they had probably come up here to overwinter before they started the spring roundup.

As only three men were walking down to the valley and there were four horses, it seemed obvious that there was another man still inside the cabin. If only all four of them had left for a while she knew she could go in for her gun and possibly some food.

Steve had taken the horses for the wagon and she was without one for herself. There were only the four horses on which the men had ridden in. Once they were all safely back inside the cabin then perhaps she could saddle one of them up and ride out to meet Steve.

After about an hour the three men returned to the cabin. They were all tall men and looked fit and strong. They needed to be in their line of work. Kelly knew she would not stand a chance of getting out of their clutches if they had a mind to molest her. She had no intention of risking a confrontation and decided to wait until dusk, or, if they were outside on the porch until dark, then at first light in the morning.

After a while all four men came out of the cabin and made their way to the lean-to barn which was almost opposite to where Kelly was hiding.

They went inside and investigated the sundry items that were stacked away. There were several bunks and straw-filled mattresses, all of which were slit.

'It looks as if someone's been searching for something here,' remarked Jesse.

The others looked at him.

'The outlaws' loot?' Johnny suggested.

35

'Could well be.' Jesse nodded. 'I wonder if they found anything?'

'Mebbe they did,' said Joel. 'That's perhaps why they left here – to spend it!'

Jude smiled. 'If that's the case, it seems a mighty big coincidence they left just before we got here. The coffee pot was still warm so they couldn't have left much before we arrived.'

'Yeah,' Joel agreed. 'I reckon we would've seen them along the way to Hazelworth. There's a rail station there and it's the nearest town from here.'

'They could have made for somewhere else,' Jesse said. 'In the opposite direction, mebbe?'

'What else have we got here?' Johnny rummaged around in a corner and came up with a box of tools. 'These might come in handy.'

'I don't know,' Jesse said slowly, and rubbed his chin thoughtfully. 'There's something here that don't quite add up. The trouble is, I don't know what it is.'

'I think I know what you mean, Jesse.' Johnny nodded. 'I don't know about you others, but I feel someone's watching us.'

'That must be the part-Indian in you, Johnny.' Jesse grinned. 'I think we'd better take a look around outside to make sure no

36

one takes a quick shot at us.'

Kelly saw them come out of the barn and inched her way further around the back of the privy. She guessed their intention and wondered where best she could hide herself. It came to her. They had already inspected the barn; if they moved further away then she would hide in there. She doubted they would search the place again.

But what if they decided to make use of the bunks and mattresses? Kelly sighed and decided perhaps she ought to hide herself somewhere else. But where?

'There wasn't anyone down by the rock pool,' Joel pointed out.

'No.' Jesse shook his head. 'I wonder whose those two graves were down there?'

'They looked quite fresh to me. One fresher than the other,' said Jude.

'You're getting quite talkative lately, Jude. What's come over you?' Jesse joked.

Jude smiled back at him. He was never offended by anything the others said.

'We'll take a walk this way and see if anyone's hiding in those trees,' was Jesse's suggestion.

Kelly watched them carefully. Once out of view she ran across to the cabin and looked for her gun. It was not there! There was no time to search for it so she snatched up some biscuits she had made the day before, eating one of them as she left the cabin cautiously and putting the others in a pocket in her dress.

Kelly considered two options now. Should she run to the corral, jump on one of the already saddled horses and ride out of here now, or should she wait until the men had turned in for the night? But if she did the latter, it would be too dangerous crossing the mountain track in the dark. It was bad enough in daylight.

She took a quick look in the direction the men had gone. There was no sign of them. She would mount up now, she decided. She was nearer the corral than they were so it would give her a few minutes at least to make her getaway.

She ran. The corral was not far from the cabin but somehow it seemed much further away than usual. Which horse to choose? The smallest would be more suitable, but would it be the fastest? she wondered. In the end she picked the black one, for senti-mental reasons, she supposed. She used to own a black mare and Jim had picked her out a black one after he and Hankins went into a town for one for her after they had pushed the prison wagon over the ravine.

Kelly untied the black gelding and mounted up. It was a bigger horse than she was used to and wearing a dress did not help matters. She usually wore men's pants and shirt for riding.

As she reached the two boulders at the start of the track she took a quick look behind her. She was sure she had not been seen. Kelly urged her new mount on but let it take its time crossing the treacherous track. She always found herself holding her breath until she reached the other side.

Once she and her mount were on flatter ground, she urged it on – on through the ruins of Larkinton and out through the exit at the other end of the town. Here she kicked the horse's flanks with her heels and it cantered away. The trouble was, she was riding a horse previously ridden by a six-foot man and she was five foot four. The stirrups were far too long and she was unable to keep her feet in them. If she did not stop and adjust them soon, then she knew she might have an accident. To fall off a horse at this stage in her pregnancy could prove fatal for the baby – and herself.

The four men came out of the copse and

made their way towards the cabin.

'Waal,' drawled Jesse, 'no sign of anyone around. I guess they've left here.'

'Seems like it,' Johnny agreed.

Joel stopped suddenly in his tracks.

'Yeah, someone's left all right – on my horse!'

The others stopped also and looked to where Joel was pointing. His black gelding was missing, the other three mounts waiting patiently to either be unsaddled or ridden.

'Lend me your horse, Jude, and I'll go fetch it back,' suggested Joel.

'No, you stay here, boys – *I'll* go,' said Jesse. 'Knowing your temper, Joel, if you catch up with whoever it is, you're likely to shoot him.'

'Huh!' Joel scoffed. 'It's you who'll most likely get shot. It's my horse, so I'll be the one to go.'

'While we stand here arguing about it, they're getting further away. Just shut up and stay here!' Jesse ordered. Hearing the tone of his voice, none of them considered further argument.

CHAPTER FIVE

It had taken five precious minutes for Kelly to adjust the stirrups to her own length. As she remounted she took a quick look behind her. Her heart skipped a beat when she saw a rider in the distance coming at full gallop towards her.

Kelly kicked her mount hard with her heels and the animal lurched forward, its strength taking her by surprise for a moment as she was used to a smaller, less powerful animal.

She rode like the wind, her long hair blowing out behind her. It felt great to begin with, but as the minutes passed, she began to wish she could slow down, stop for a while, even. But she dared not. She was sure the man following her was one of the four at Paradise, and when he caught up with her she was fearful of how he would treat her for stealing one of their horses. What if he took the animal from her and abandoned her miles from anywhere? What if he...? She dared not finish her thoughts. She would be at his mercy.

41

Kelly took another quick look behind her and was even more fearful as the distance between them was lessening. Tears gathered in her eyes as she realized it was hopeless to continue with this race. The outcome was obvious and the constant jogging was making her feel faint and ill.

Now she could hear clearly the hoofbeats of the pursuing animal behind her. She dug in her heels to urge the gelding to greater speed. It managed it for a while, but soon she knew the game was up.

Then she heard a whirring sound in the air. In another second she felt the coil of a lariat around her shoulders and arms. She tried to pull the rope off her but it was tightening around her all the time and she felt herself being pulled backwards. Kelly knew that at all costs she must not fall from the horse. Her fears were for her unborn baby more than herself. She held on to the pommel of the saddle with both hands and a moment or two later her pursuer had come level with her. He twirled the rope round and round her body and she felt like a trussed-up chicken.

Both horses stopped and the man alighted from his mount.

'Kick your feet free of the stirrups!' he ordered.

Kelly knew there was nothing she could do but obey. She found herself being lifted easily to the ground. He held her for a while as he looked down at her.

'Waal, you're quite a beauty, ain't yer?' He smiled, his blue eyes twinkling and the corners of them creasing in amusement.

Kelly looked up at him and the man saw both fear and defiance in her hazel eyes.

'They hang horse-thieves you know,' he told her.

Kelly wriggled a little under the ropes; she felt completely helpless.

'Don't worry, I ain't gonna hurt yer. What's yer name?' Jesse asked.

There was no reply; Kelly just looked down, defeated.

Jesse unwound the coils that bound her, then recoiled the rope and replaced it on his saddle pommel.

'Why did you ride off like that?' Jesse asked her.

There was no reply.

'Not talking, huh? Waal, I'll find out some-time. Go on, get aboard again and we'll go back.'

Kelly felt in no condition to ride any further at the moment and promptly sat down on the ground.

'I said get back on that horse, miss!'

She looked up at him, still not speaking, and put her head in her hands.

Jesse sighed. 'OK, you can have a bit of a rest for a while.' He sat down beside her. 'Who are you and what were you doing up there in the hills on your own?'

Kelly refused to answer him.

'I've got a friend who don't say above two words all day. He does answer when he spoken to though. My name's Jesse. Are you gonna tell me yours?'

Kelly kept silent.

'OK, you've had a breather. Now get on that horse!'

When she did not do as she was told Jesse stood up and pulled her to a standing position beside him. Kelly wasted no time: she kicked the man hard on his shins.

She saw his eyes watering at the pain she had inflicted and as he moved towards her she held up her arms to deflect the blow she expected from him.

'I ain't gonna hit you – but my golly you deserve it!' Jesse told her bitterly. The next moment Kelly found herself being picked up and put on the horse's saddle. She did not give Jesse time to mount his own horse before she had kicked her mount in the ribs and they were off again.

Jesse remounted in an instant and was after her.

'It won't do you no good, lady. You might as well come back here now!'

They both rode a good few yards before Jesse drew up alongside her and caught hold of the reins of her horse.

'You're going the wrong way,' he told her, as if she didn't know. 'Enough of this nonsense, girl, or I'll tan your backside, see if I don't.'

It was no use. Kelly felt completely exhausted and allowed herself to be led back towards Larkinton.

The journey back was silent on Kelly's part and she could tell Jesse was becoming slightly annoyed with her.

'Not very good company, are you?' he said at last when every attempt he made to start a conversation failed.

'Are you a mute or something?' he asked her.

Kelly turned her head sideways and looked him straight in those blue eyes of his. She gave him a small smile and looked straight ahead of her again.

'Mebbe the boys will get you to talk,' he said. 'Joel, the feller whose horse you stole, won't be too friendly towards you. He's got a bit of a temper on him has that one. He's got almost the same colour hair as you, too. I bet you've got a temper at times.'

Kelly continued riding with Jesse still holding the reins of her mount.

'It'll be getting dark soon,' Jesse remarked. 'You'd better hope that we reach that ledge while we can still see, otherwise it means a night out in the open. If you hadn't played tag all that time we could have been sure of getting back in daylight. So if we do spend the night out in the open, then it'll be all your fault!' Jesse grumbled.

It wouldn't be the first time, Kelly thought to herself. She'd spent nights under the stars with the whole Bassett gang and also alone with Jim. Dear Jim. She still thought of him constantly. Tears came into her eyes at the thought of the one special time they had shared a blanket and he had made love to her so wonderfully. But she loved Steve even more. If only he was back with her now.

She began to worry about the man called Joel, whose horse she had stolen. She hoped Jesse would not allow him to hurt her. He seemed as if he was the leader of the three men and he reminded her a bit of Hay Bassett. He had the same physique, tall,

46

broad-shouldered, with hard muscles under his shirt. He also spoke like Hay: his voice was low and his words came slowly, sparingly, with an air of authority about them. This man riding beside her now though, wore a light-brown droopy moustache, the same colour as his hair, whereas Hay was usually clean-shaven.

It had become dark within minutes and Kelly knew her bed that night would be on the hard ground instead of her comfortable mattress. But if she had reached Paradise before nightfall, what then? Where would all the men sleep? She was used to sharing the cabin with several men, but those there now were unknown to her. She had been safe before because Hay Bassett had told his men they would have him to deal with if any of them had touched her in any way.

'Dismount now,' Jesse told her, breaking into her thoughts. 'We can't ride any further tonight.'

Kelly was about to dismount but Jesse was soon standing beside her horse and he lifted her down. Her heartbeats quickened when he held her a few moments longer and looked down at her barely discernible face.

'You'd better not kick me again, young lady, or you'll wish you hadn't. Savvy?'

Kelly nodded in the semi-darkness and he saw the movement of her head.

'Now make yourself comfortable while I put down the bed rolls.'

Kelly returned to him a few moments later and saw that the bedding was close together.

'If you promise me you won't try and ride off in the night I won't tie you up. Do you promise?' he asked her.

Kelly did not reply or nod so Jesse unsaddled both horses and placed each saddle at the head of the laid-out bed rolls for a pillow. He uncoiled his lariat and wound it around her waist several times, looping one end through the coils and tying a knot that would be difficult to undo.

'Take your boots off then get between the blankets. I'll have the other end of this rope around my arm so I'll know if you intend riding off in the night.'

Kelly did as he asked and pulled the blankets up high over her ears.

'Good night. Sleep well,' he said and turned his back on her.

Kelly smiled in the darkness. At least he did not intend her any harm, which was one consolation. After a while she was asleep.

When she woke the next morning at early

light she found that Jesse had saddled his own horse and was waiting for her to wake up.

'Come on, out of there!' he said, pulling the saddle away from under her head and throwing it on to the back of Joel's horse. 'I'll give you a couple of minutes, then we get going.'

A few minutes later Kelly went to mount up but Jesse picked her up in his strong arms and placed her in the saddle.

'Are you gonna talk to me today?' he asked as they moved off.

Kelly considered it for a moment, then shook her head.

'Most women can't stop talking. Yackety-yackety-yack! It makes a real change to meet a silent one.'

Kelly smiled slightly. She was beginning to take to this man at her side. She felt safe with him. She just hoped he'd keep her safe from his friends.

When they reached the narrow track leading to Paradise, Kelly stopped while still on the wider part.

'Jesse,' she began.

'Oh, so you can talk. What is it?' he asked her.

'Jesse, will you make sure the others don't

hurt me?'

He smiled a little, realizing that she was afraid of them, which was most likely the reason why she'd tried to escape the day before.

'My shins tell me that you are quite able to take care of yourself, young woman,' said Jesse, who could still feel the pain from her booted onslaught.

'I'm real sorry about that,' she said.' You see...' she faltered, '...I'm gonna have a baby.'

Jesse's mouth opened slightly.

'Where's your man?' Jesse asked her.

Kelly realized that he meant the father of her baby, but Kelly had no intention of telling him about Hay Bassett and his gang.

'He's gone to fetch supplies to see us through the winter. He'll be back in three days' time.'

'Is it him you were riding off to find?' Jesse asked her.

'Yes. I didn't feel safe here with you all. Please say you'll protect me from them,' she pleaded.

'You have my word, ma'am. And Jesse's word is his bond.' He let her go first across the track and began to wish that he had let her ride on to meet her man. If it wasn't for Joel's horse, he probably would have done.

Jesse had a feeling that things could be rather awkward with a woman amongst four men.

CHAPTER SIX

Kelly and Jesse drew up outside the cabin where the three men were sitting on the porch steps in the morning sun.

Kelly sat astride her horse and looked down at them, trying to weigh up their characters from their faces. None of them looked particularly fearsome close to.

Jesse dismounted and lifted Kelly down. Joel stood up and came forward.

'This here's your horse-thief, Joel,' said Jesse.

'A woman!' Joel exclaimed

'You're getting quite observant.' Jesse grinned.

'They hang horse-thieves,' Joel growled at her.

'I've already told her that,' said Jesse.

'I've a good mind to teach you a lesson,' Joel told her, his face as black as thunder.

Kelly instinctively held her arms up in

front of her face to ward off any blow.

Jesse came between them. 'You'll do no such thing,' he announced. 'All of you, if anyone lays a finger on this woman, you'll have me to answer to. I'm not a violent man as you know, but I won't stand by and let any man hurt a woman. Do you hear me?' His voice rose slightly with the last sentence.

They all murmured that they had heard him.

'Seems like she's used to being hit,' Johnny Diamond remarked.

Jesse nodded. 'She acted the same with me. She knows now that I wouldn't hurt her. She's not much of a talker.'

'What's your name?' Joel asked her.

Kelly looked up at the tall man before her. He reminded her of Sandy Kaye but this man was a bit taller than Sandy had been. She ignored him and started up the two steps to the cabin.

Joel pulled her around by her arm to face him and immediately regretted it when Kelly kicked him hard on his left shinbone. The man hopped back a pace and held on to his injured leg, letting out an oath at the same time.

'Oh,' said Jesse, a twinkle in his eye, 'I forgot to warn you. She kicks.' He laughed loudly at Joel's discomfort, knowing full well how the red-headed man felt, for his own shin was still hurting from the day before.

As Kelly entered the cabin she was greeted by the familiar cool darkness of the large room. She could smell coffee and she realized that she had not eaten since the morning before, not even the few biscuits she had put in the pocket of her dress before she rode off on Joel's horse. She had only had a small drop of water from the canteen that hung on the animal's saddle pommel as it was almost empty. She felt terribly weak at that moment and suddenly everything went black.

Joel was the first to get to her as she lay on the floor. He picked her up gently and carried her across to the bed where he put her down. Jesse noticed the concerned expression on his friend's face as he looked down at her.

'What's wrong with her, Jesse?' Joel asked the older man.

'She must be weak from hunger and thirst I reckon. And another thing – she's expecting.'

'Expecting what?' asked Jude.

'A baby, you fool! What else?' Jesse admonished.

Jude nodded, feeling stupid at his question.

'What's the story?' Joel asked.

Jesse sighed and shrugged his broad shoulders. 'As I said, she hasn't spoken much – nothing at all until we reached the far side of the track in here. She made me promise I'd not let you others touch her and I intend keeping my word. She also told me she was expecting a baby. I don't know how far gone she is though.'

'What about you, did you touch her last night, Jesse?' Joel demanded to know.

Jesse gave him a withering look. 'I tied a rope around her waist and around my arm so I'd get a good night's sleep without having to worry about losing your horse again. She's no saloon-girl, Joel. She's got a man, she don't need another.'

When Kelly opened her eyes she was lying on her bed in the far corner of the room. All four men were looking down at her. She sucked in her breath in sudden fear.

'Here you are, ma'am.' It was Jude, the quiet one. 'Have a drink of this coffee, it might make you feel better.'

Kelly sat up on the bed, took the mug from his large hand and gave him a smile of thanks.

'We've got some food cooked,' Johnny Diamond told her. 'Can you come up to the table for it?'

Their voices were kind and concerned about her and Kelly began to feel a little safer. Jesse had promised her that he would keep her safe from these men and she had a feeling he would keep his word to her.

When she had finished the coffee she walked across to the long table and sat down on one of the long forms.

A plate of food was promptly put before her and also one for Jesse who was almost as hungry as she was. The meal consisted of strips cut off a dried side of bacon and some beans. Kelly guessed the men must have brought the bacon with them as she knew she and Steve were completely out of it.

'That was good,' she pronounced after she had eaten it all.

'Not bad, Jude.' Jesse nodded at the man he guessed was the cook.

'We still don't know your name, ma'am,' Jesse reminded her.

Kelly thought for a few seconds. She did not want to reveal her true identity in case they had heard about her involvement with the Bassett gang and her trial.

'Jean,' she answered, the only name to

come into her head. It had been the name of her stepmother who had died in childbirth. The baby boy had died also. This was the cause of Denver Branch's madness through grief at the double loss of his wife and son. He had blamed Kelly as she had been at the river with Steve when Jean had gone into labour. Kelly knew her stepfather already hated her for being the cause of the death of her own mother when she was born, and that Kelly was not Denver's daughter. In his anger he had cut her hair short and made her dress as a boy to make up for the son he had lost. It was soon afterwards that the Bassett gang arrived at their home with a wounded man after a bank raid in the nearby town of Mayville. After a shoot-out with the posse, Denver Branch forced Kelly to join the Bassett gang with him and his two men. The gang were unaware of Kelly's true sex to begin with, and only found out after she was forced to fight Sandy Kaye, the youngest of the gang, with fists.

She was brought back to the present by Jesse speaking.

It all seemed such a long time ago, but was only about seven months.

'Well, Jean,' Jesse began, breaking into her thoughts, 'this red-headed one is Joel –

whose horse you stole.'

'I'm sorry, Joel, but I was afraid of you all.'

'Forget it,' he answered.

'And these other two are Jude, the quiet one I told you about, and Johnny.'

Kelly nodded. 'What are your intentions?' she asked. 'How long do you intend sticking around here?'

'Waal, we had hoped to stay here for the winter. We thought this place was deserted. But now we know it ain't, waal, I don't know what we're gonna do. We came here also to look for the Bassett gang's loot.'

Jesse studied the girl's face at his last words. Did she know anything about the hidden money? If she did, her face did not show it. Maybe she was a good poker-player, he thought.

'Steve and I have heard of them. We even looked around ourselves for the loot, but we didn't find anything.'

'Are you tellin' me the truth?' Jesse asked her, scrutinizing her face intently. 'We noticed those mattresses in the barn – every one slit. Did you find anything in any of them?'

'We completely cleared this cabin – turfed everything outside – and gave it a good clean. We put the bunks the Bassett gang must have slept on in the barn to use as fuel throughout the winter. It was only later on that we thought about the mattresses. But there was no money in any of them. We haven't been here long enough to look anywhere else. Feel free to look around for yourselves if you want to,' Kelly suggested.

'We might just do that, Jean,' Jesse said.

'What about right now?' Joel suggested.

'What about her?' Johnny Diamond asked, jerking his thumb in Kelly's direction.

'You can stay here with her, Johnny,' Jesse said, 'just in case she decides to leave on one of our horses again.'

Kelly stood up from the table and faced Jesse, her lips set firm.

'That won't be necessary, Jesse. I couldn't ride any further.'

Jesse thought for a second, then said, 'You can rest up here and Johnny will look out for you. He won't touch you – or he knows what'll happen to him if he does.' Jesse looked the longhaired man straight in the eyes.

The men had noticed a couple of shovels in the barn the day before. Three of them went to fetch them and Kelly watched as they walked towards the valley. She wondered how long they would be and whether she really would be safe with this half-breed Indian.

Kelly decided to start on some sewing for the baby and sat on a chair on the stoop with her sewing things.

Johnny sat on the bottom step below her, cleaning his gun with his bandanna. It did not seem as if he had anything to say and the two remained silent for about ten minutes.

'Does your man beat you?' Johnny asked at last.

Kelly smiled at the suggestion. 'Of course not! We love each other very much indeed.'

'Then why did you act like you were used to being hit by a man when you first came here this morning?'

'By the look on Joel's face, I just expected that's what he would do. My stepfather beat me often.'

Johnny looked up at her from his seat on the step and Kelly could see pity in his eyes for her.

'Is he still alive?' he asked her.

'No. No one I used to know is still alive,' she said a little wistfully. 'All gone, except for Steve.'

'I've got nobody either. Jesse and the others are my family now,' he volunteered.

'Jesse seems a nice man,' said Kelly. 'A man you could really trust.'

'Yeah.' Johnny nodded. 'There's no one better than Jesse. The other two are good men as well. We've been riding together now for two years. After a round-up is over, most cowboys go off their own separate ways, but Jesse and us three kinda stuck together. We look out for each other and would give our lives for each other.'

Kelly's eyes became misty at his words. She had never heard a man speak about others as this one had. It made a real change from the men she had met in her life before, Steve excluded, who only thought of themselves and what they could take.

They talked quite easily together for the rest of the afternoon. Kelly listened more than she was prepared to talk. She knew she must not reveal anything about herself that would give the game away about who she really was.

'Have you lived with your man long?' Johnny asked her.

'Two weeks,' Kelly replied, then realized how it sounded. If she and Steve had only lived together for two weeks then she would not know if she was pregnant now.

'Two weeks up here, that is,' she quickly

60

added. 'I've known him for about five or six months.'

'You're not married,' he stated.

'No,' she shook her head, 'but we feel married.'

'Yeah, you would do, you expecting and all,' said Johnny. 'I'd like a woman of my own,' he added.

'I expect you'll find one at some time.' Kelly smiled at him.

He turned his unusually violet-coloured eyes on her and returned the smile.

'I doubt it. I'm in between two camps,' he said. 'I'm neither white nor Indian. Neither kind wants the likes of me.'

'You'll find someone,' Kelly repeated. 'You're a nice-looking man.' She turned her eyes back to her sewing but she could tell he was still looking at her. She hoped her words had not given him the impression that she was leading him on.

About five in the afternoon, Jesse and the others returned. Jude and Joel threw the shovels down at Johnny's feet, their faces betraying their feelings of disappointment.

'No luck, I gather?' said Johnny.

'Nah.' Jesse shook his head in disgust. 'We dug up those two mounds near the rock pool. One of the bodies looked quite fresh.

Been dead no more than two weeks, I reckon.' He looked directly at Kelly whose face had gone ashen. 'Any idea who the feller was, Jean?' he asked her.

Kelly shook her head, blinking away the tears that had come into her eyes.

'I'll go and make some coffee,' she said, turning away from them quickly.

All four men looked at her retreating figure and looked at each other.

'That girl knows more than she's lettin' on,' said Jesse. 'I reckon we'd better find out what it is.'

CHAPTER SEVEN

Kelly was putting the coffee pot on the stove when the men followed her into the cabin. Jesse was first and stood beside her, his expression demanding answers.

'Who are those bodies we dug up today?' Jesse asked her.

'How should I know?' she replied, looking him straight in the eyes.

'I think you know. Now come on, girl, tell me!'

She turned away from him saying, 'Mind your own damn business!'

Jesse caught her by the arm and pulled her round to face him again, the next second receiving another kick on his shin, almost on the same spot as the first wound. She saw him wince at the pain, then found herself being picked up as if she were a feather, carried across to the bed and dumped down on it.

'Jesse!' Jude shouted after him, 'what are you gonna do to her?'

'What I should've done to start with!' he growled.

'Leave her be, Jesse!' Jude ordered. The others looked at him in surprise, for this was not the Jude they knew.

'Don't worry yourself, Jude,' said Jesse. And with that, he knelt on the top of her legs with one knee and pulled off her boots. 'There, girlie, you'll not do any more damage. You can have them back when I'm sure you can behave yourself.'

Kelly's temper had become inflamed at the injustice of it. These men were each twice her size and now she had no defence against them at all. Her hands made small fists with which she pounded on Jesse's back and arms.

Jesse's laugh made her even angrier and she beat him even harder. The others joined in the laughter.

'You all come riding in here, invading my home and demanding answers to your questions. It's time you all left. Steve will be mighty angry at you all being here!' Kelly buried her head in her pillow crying tears of anger.

Her boots were placed on the top of the cupboard out of her reach and the men got on with the coffee-making and preparing supper for them all.

'Come on, Jean – if that's your real name,' Jesse called to her as the men sat down at the table. 'Better come and eat it while it's still hot.'

Kelly contemplated ignoring the man and going without supper, but realized this would be foolish on her part. She padded over to the table and sat at one end, next to Jude. She gave the man a smile, which made his day.

After supper Jude helped her to clear away the dishes and wash and dry them on the stoop. When they came back into the room a pack of playing-cards had been produced by one of them and four hands had been dealt. Jude joined them at the table.

'I hope you've no objection to us gambling, Jean?' Jesse asked.

'As long as you don't go shooting each other over it,' Kelly told him.

'No, we won't shoot each other,' Jesse said, 'but there's been some shooting around here though, hasn't there? And I think you were around when it happened.'

Kelly's look was still defiant. 'Think what you like,' was Kelly's response. 'By the way, where are you men sleeping tonight? You're definitely not sleeping here!'

'If we leave you alone in this cabin tonight,' said Joel, 'what's to say you won't ride off on one of the horses again as soon as it gets light in the morning?'

'I could give you my word that I wouldn't,' Kelly replied.

'Sorry to have to say this, ma'am, but your word don't count fer much with me,' Joel informed her.

'Well, I can't reach my boots, and I wouldn't get far without them,' Kelly reminded him.

Jesse turned his head and looked at her as she stood beside him.

'You needn't worry that pretty little head of yours, Jean. None of us will lay a finger on you. You can sleep soundly in your bed and we'll sleep on the floor.'

Kelly knew it was no use arguing with the man. She lay down on the bed while they continued playing cards in the light of the lamp set before them on the table.

When Kelly woke the next morning she realized she had dropped off to sleep and had not heard the men retiring for the night on the floor. It was like being back with the Bassett gang, she thought to herself, except that these men made their living among cattle and horses, whereas the gang made theirs robbing banks. She knew which group she preferred to be with. The ones there now were honest and had treated her well. They even did the cooking!

The men were tucking in to breakfast when she became fully awake. She needed to go outside and to have a quick wash before she sat down with them.

'Good morning, ma'am,' said Jude whom she had sat next to again.

'Good morning, Jude.' She smiled at him.

'We'll be lookin' around again today,' Jesse said. 'Joel, I'd like you to stay here and take care of Jean while we're gone.'

'Sure, Jesse.'

'Don't I have anything to say about it?'

Kelly glowered across at Jesse, sitting opposite.

'No,' was his short reply.

Kelly ate her breakfast. She was becoming used to being cooked for and felt she might get out of the habit of cooking before Steve came home. At the thought of Steve she felt a sudden sadness at his being away from her. This was the third day of his absence and she could not wait to see him again.

Riding towards Larkinton were three men. Two of them were not suitably dressed for horseback-riding and by their appearance, in their dark suits, black shoes and derby hats could be easily taken for bank or government officials, which indeed they were. The third man was dressed more suitably in well-worn Levis, check shirt, black vest and fedora. He also wore a Colt .44 in his gun belt.

'Not far now, Mr Richards, Mr Franks,' the third man told them. He could see that the two men riding beside him looked decidedly uncomfortable and knew they would be only too pleased when they eventually dismounted at their destination. They had spent one night on the trail and Ben Frazer, who was taking care of the two men by his side, knew the experience was less than comfortable for his charges.

'Don't forget, Mr Frazer,' Franks, the shorter of the two city men began, 'if there are any people occupying the outlaws' camp in the hills, they must be evicted immediately. Do you understand me?'

There was a moment's silence before Frazer answered.

'I'm the only one amongst us with a gun, Mr Franks. If there are too many of them, it's gonna be a bit difficult.'

'You were recommended to us, Frazer. They told us you were the best – that you've done this type of work before.'

'True,' Frazer replied. 'But if it's a couple, a woman, do you still want me to throw them off the place? Winter's coming.'

Franks was adamant. 'You've been paid to do a job, Mr Frazer, and we want it done. That place must be cleared of people before we start our investigations. There is money stashed away up there somewhere – money stolen from many banks in Colorado – and it's our job to find it. The insurance companies won't hand over a penny to the banks that have been robbed until we've done our best to find that outlaw Bassett's loot.'

Frazer looked ahead of him as he rode. He

wondered why he was questioning the decisions of these two men. He was being well paid for guarding the two and also for evicting anyone who had taken over the cabin in the place called Paradise. He decided to put any qualms he might have aside and just do his job. He also realized he might have quite a bit of digging to do once they arrived in the mountain hideout.

As Jesse, Jude and Johnny left the cabin, Joel followed them outside.

'Can I trust you to keep your hands off the girl?' Jesse asked him.

'Sure, Jesse. She'll be safe with me,' Joel promised.

'I hope so, Joel. If I find you've hurt her in any way I'll ... waal, I hope I won't have to,' Jesse finished.

'You're mighty fond of that girl, ain't yer?' Joel grinned.

Jesse smiled back at him. 'She's got spirit, I'll say that. I like horses and women with spirit. It gives a man satisfaction to tame 'em. Pity her man's coming back soon. I wouldn't mind having a go at taming her – even if I am old enough to be her pa.'

'Where are we digging today, Jesse?' Johnny Diamond asked.

'Down by the rock pool and a bit further. There's a forest half a mile away from there, and there are other spots that we could look at. I rather hoped we'd find something in those graves yesterday. We'll take the horses, they could use the exercise,' he decided, and Joel walked with them to the corral.

'I wouldn't mind coming along with you. I'm not cut out for child-minding,' Joel scowled.

'Some child!' Johnny laughed.

Kelly came to the cabin door and watched the men walk over to the corral. She thought quickly. While they were gone she would get hold of her boots – and look for her gun.

Satisfied that she would have a few moments alone, Kelly grabbed a chair, stood on tiptoe and dropped her boots down to the floor. She could see her gun belt right at the back, which brought a smile to her face. She took the gun out of its holster and checked the chamber. It was fully loaded. She quickly got down off the chair and put it back in the position it had been in before. She donned her boots and hid the gun under the mattress. Kelly had contemplated putting the gun in the pocket of her dress, but she knew it would be too heavy and would be noticed.

Her eyes went to the table and she considered removing the hidden legacy from Doc Reynolds, but she knew there would not be time before Joel returned; it was safe enough for the moment where it was. Once he noticed she was wearing her boots, he would know that she had also found her gun on the top of the cupboard.

Ten minutes later Joel walked in to find Kelly making biscuits.

'So you can cook?' Joel remarked. 'We haven't seen much of it since we've been here.'

Kelly allowed him a small smile. 'No, it's been quite a welcome change for me, being cooked for. There's a haunch of venison hanging up in the barn. If you'd bring it to me I'll make stew – or maybe a pie.'

Joel nodded. 'OK.' He hesitated, wondering what was different about her since he'd last seen her some minutes ago. It would not come to him at first, but as he walked towards the barn it suddenly occurred to him that she was wearing her boots. And if she'd found her boots, then she would have found the gun!

CHAPTER EIGHT

Joel quickly lifted the venison, which was wrapped in sacking, from a hook and hurried back to the cabin. He drew his gun, bent down under the window and cautiously looked in. Kelly was still making biscuits, arranging the circles of mixture onto a flat tray ready for the oven beside the stove. He could not see a gun nearby.

He quietly opened the door, his .44 still in his hand, and stood in the doorway. Her face looked shocked at the sight of the gun.

'What do you think you're doing?' she asked him, eyeing the weapon.

'What have you done with the gun you found on the cupboard?'

'Gun?' she queried.

'Don't play games with me, girl! Where is it?'

'A girl's gotta have some protection,' Kelly told him. 'You others have each got a gun, so why can't I have one?'

'Guns aren't made for women. Why, I don't suppose you even know how to use one.'

Kelly frowned. 'No. I really must learn some day. You never know when one might come in useful. Perhaps you'd like to teach me, Joel?' She looked up at him coquettishly.

'You shouldn't go playing around with loaded guns, Jean. You might have an accident and shoot yourself – or someone else – by mistake. Now come on, where is it?'

'Do you know, I've quite forgotten. Now enough about guns. Would you skin that deer for me please – and cut it up into pieces? I don't like sharp knives – I could have an accident.'

She smiled up at him mockingly.

Joel replaced the gun in its holster, sighing a little at the way she had gotten round him.

'OK. I'll find the gun afterwards. I don't reckon you'd shoot me anyway.'

Mr Richards, Mr Franks and Ben Frazer were within view of the entrance to Larkinton. Frazer urged his mount on so that he would lead the way through the mouth of the box canyon.

'There's not a single building left untouched by the blaze,' Richards remarked unnecessarily. 'Should we not be looking around here first before we go on to Paradise?'

73

'I reckon others have beaten us to it, Mr Richards,' Frazer replied. 'We might also be going on a wild-goose chase to Paradise, too.'

'But I thought you said that the narrow track would deter most people from going any further than this?'

Ben Frazer nodded. 'I said "most" people, Mr Richards. You will always get those with a bit more guts than others and who are more determined to try their luck, in spite of the risks.'

Franks had not joined in the conversation as yet. The reminder that they had not reached the most dangerous part of this expedition was making his stomach churn.

They rode on for two miles until they reached the narrow track leading to Paradise.

'My God, Frazer!' Franks exclaimed. 'We can't ride over there! Just look at the drop!'

A smirk appeared on Frazer's lips at the Easterner's words.

'Mr Franks,' Frazer began, 'a seventeen-year-old girl rode over this track – and she had been badly beaten up by one of the gang. She was in no condition to ride at all, let alone across here – yet she did!'

Franks could feel the admiration for the

girl in Frazer's voice and he suddenly felt the coward he really was.

'Just let your horse find its own way, Mr Franks,' Frazer advised. 'I've found that horses are more reliable than most men I've met.'

The cutting edge to his words was not lost on the two men following behind their guide.

'Lead on then, Mr Frazer!' Franks ordered.

Franks gallantly allowed his partner, Richards to precede him. When it was his turn to start over the track, Franks felt the vomit which had been churning at the pit of his stomach, leave his mouth. His heart was beating hard within his chest and at that moment he was wishing himself many miles away from this place.

Frazer stopped once he had passed by the boulders on each side of the track at the other end and looked at the two men he was guiding. Franks was visibly shaking and for a brief moment Frazer actually pitied the man. Richards, although equally worried about his experience of a moment ago, showed his fear less noticeably. Frazer guessed this man was made of sterner stuff than his associate.

Frazer looked ahead of him at the cabin.

Smoke was coming from the chimney, so the place was obviously occupied.

'There's only one horse in the corral,' said Frazer, 'so we shouldn't have too much trouble evicting them from here. We'll ride in from our left, past the corral, and hope that they won't have seen us from the window by the time we reach the door.'

'Very well, Frazer.' Richards nodded. 'But when we get there you will have to be firm and make sure they obey the eviction notice you'll serve on them.'

'Leave it to me, Mr Richards. They'll go, don't worry.'

Franks allowed the other two men to lead the way. When they reached the corral, they dismounted at Frazer's hand signals, tied their mounts to the corral fence and went the rest of the way to the cabin on foot.

When they reached it, Frazer motioned for the men to stand to one side of the door while he crept to the window and cautiously looked inside. He could see a tall, red-headed man standing next to a slightly built woman at the long table in the centre of the room. She was watching the man cutting up some meat.

Frazer slowly pushed the door open with his foot and stood in the doorway, his Colt revolver in his hand.

'Put your hands up, both of you!' he demanded.

Both were taken completely by surprise at the sudden intrusion. Then they noticed two other men in city clothes appear in the doorway and follow the first man inside the room.

'Take his gun, Mr Richards!' Frazer said over his shoulder.

The taller of the two city men moved forward and removed Joel's gun from its holster, holding it by the trigger guard as if fearful that it would suddenly explode of its own accord. He passed the weapon to his associate, who was equally appalled at holding such a dangerous object.

'I'm hereby serving an eviction notice on you,' said Frazer to Joel. 'What's your name, mister?'

Joel ignored this question. 'You've no right doing this!' he said, raising his voice in anger. 'You don't own this land – no one does. We're claiming squatters' rights.'

'Shut up!' Frazer told him. 'What's your name to go on this form?'

'Jesse James – or is it Billy the Kid?' Joel replied with a smirk on his face.

The smirk was quickly wiped off by a

punch on his mouth from Frazer, who turned his attention to Kelly.

'What's his name?' he asked, ignoring Joel's split lip, which was bleeding quite a lot.

'Do you know, I've completely forgotten,' said Kelly. 'It must be this mountain air, it does funny things to a person's brain.'

Frazer's face was dark with anger.

'Don't go getting smart with me, young woman. I don't make a habit of hitting women, but I can make an exception in your case if you don't give me a straight answer. Now, who is this feller – and who are you?'

'I don't know,' Kelly smiled. 'He just rode in one day and we haven't had time to get introduced properly. I think he's lost his memory.'

Kelly was not prepared for the man's large hand across her face and the force of it knocked her to the floor.

'You low down stinking dog!' Joel exclaimed, moving forward towards the man.

Frazer pushed the barrel of his gun into Joel's stomach and the sound of the gun being cocked stopped him in his tracks.

'One more word out of you and I'll have no hesitation in using this. Now, tell me your name so I can get this eviction order served, and be quick about it!'

Kelly shook her head to clear it after the blow and sat up, supporting herself by both hands on the floor.

'Don't kill him!' Kelly implored. 'His name's John – John Murphy. He's my husband,' Kelly lied.

Frazer looked at Joel. 'Is that right?' he asked.

'Sure,' Joel answered and looked down at Kelly in surprise. 'You OK, honey?' he asked her solicitously.

'Yes, darling, I'm all right – I think. I'll just lie down on the bed for a while. I don't want anything to happen to the baby.'

Frazer looked at them both. 'What baby?'

Joel glowered down at the gun still pointing at his stomach.

'The baby she's expectin' of course! You can't evict us now. How will we manage with the baby coming and all?'

'That's not our problem, mister. Now get your belongings and get out!'

By now Kelly had reached the bed and while the two were talking she managed to secrete the gun in her dress pocket, although it stuck out and Kelly had to hold her arm over it.

'Just how do you expect us to do that, mister?' Kelly asked of Frazer. 'We've only got the one horse between us. And how on earth are we to carry everything?'

'As I said, it's not our problem. My job was to serve you with a notice and I've done it.'

Richards stepped forward. 'Your job, Mr Frazer is not only to serve the notice, but see to it that the eviction is carried out. You're wasting time. We want to be out of here at the end of two weeks. We don't want to be here when winter sets in.'

The search for the Bassett gang's loot had proved unfruitful. All three men were disappointed, tired and hungry. They had searched in every place they could think of – round the boulder by the rock pool, along the edge of the pool and all round the base of the lone tree. It looked as if it had been used for target practice from the many bullet holes in the white ring half-way up, where a branch had fallen off years before. Jesse had even climbed up the tree and looked among the branches. He found that the trunk was completely hollow. It would have been a good place to hide a sack or box of money, but this idea was out of the question, as how was anyone to get at it if it was at the bottom – apart from chopping the tree down, of course? This might have to be done, though, if the money was not found anywhere else. They rode over to the forest about half a mile from this spot but despite looking around for any likely places, they came away empty-handed.

They made their way back to the cabin and Jesse had the feeling his two companions were cursing him for his bright idea of coming up here having come to nothing.

As they reached the spring where they obtained their water supply Jesse looked over towards the corral. Besides Joel's horse inside the corral, there were three horses tied to the outside.

'Look!' Jesse pointed to the others, 'We've got company.'

CHAPTER NINE

Jesse was certain none of the riders would be the girl's man, Steve, for he had left with a wagon. He did not think he would bring anyone back with him. Were the three riders lawmen or cowboys like themselves, hoping to overwinter in the cabin? Maybe they had come in search of the Bassett gang's loot as well? If so, then they would hardly welcome the presence of men of like mind.

'What do we do, Jesse?' Johnny asked their leader.

'Waal, I reckon we'd better approach the place slow – keep to the left by the corral and look through the window before going in.'

The other two nodded in agreement and tried to keep to the left of the window as much as possible.

They tied their mounts alongside the three waiting there already and crept slowly towards the cabin.

Jesse peered in and could see Joel standing before a man with a gun in his hand. Two other men in city clothes were standing to one side looking like a couple of fish out of water. Kelly – or Jean as he knew her – was by the bed. He wondered if she had been hurt in any way and Jesse was surprised to find his hackles rising at the thought of any man harming her and surprise too, that this slip of a girl could affect him so much.

Jesse waited a while. Jean was starting to walk slowly towards the men, her arm somewhat stiff by her side. What was wrong with her? Jesse wondered.

'Oh, my biscuits!' Kelly said in alarm. 'They must be almost burnt to a cinder!' She hurried around the table to the oven and took a cloth to hold the tin of smoking biscuits.

'Oh look, they're all spoilt!' Kelly almost wailed.

'Never mind the stupid biscuits,' Frazer growled. 'Collect what belongings you can carry and get out!'

Kelly was still holding the hot tin as she walked up to the man. 'Would you like to try one?' she asked with a small smile on her lips.

'No, I wouldn't! Now hurry it up and get out!'

Kelly moved even nearer. 'Go on, try one,' she said, and while his eyes were taken away from Joel, Kelly used the baking tin to swipe the gun from his hand. It clattered to the floor and Joel made a lunge for it.

'Not so fast, mister!' The voice came from one of the city men, Richards. He held Joel's gun which Frazer had handed to him earlier and they could all see the man's hand shaking slightly. They also noticed that the gun had not been cocked.

Things happened quickly then. Kelly drew her gun out of her dress pocket and cocked it as she was bringing it up level.

'Put your gun down, mister!' she ordered 'or I'll use this on you. I'm not joking.'

Richards tried to pull the trigger and was shocked when nothing happened.

Kelly kicked him hard on the shins, relieving him of the gun at the same time. She now had two guns, one in each hand. She cocked the one in her left hand with more difficulty and handed it over to Joel.

'Pick this feller's gun up, Joel, while I cover him!' Kelly ordered.

At this point Jesse led the way through the cabin door. His blue eyes were twinkling and his face was smiling.

'We sure underestimated you, Jean, and that's a fact!' he exclaimed. 'Who are these fellers?'

'They've come to evict us, Jesse,' Kelly told him. 'I reckon they know now that we're in no mood to be evicted. What shall we do with them?' she asked.

'Kick 'em up the backside and send them on their way.'

Jude and Johnny were standing in the doorway, puzzled, surprise and admiration showing on their faces at the sight of this small young woman before them.

'Who are you men?' Frazer demanded.

'Just cowboys overwintering,' Jesse answered.

'This makes no difference.' The man's eyes were blazing in anger. 'I've served an eviction notice and you are legally obliged to leave here – right now!'

'Oh shut up!' said Kelly a little wearily. 'The notice ain't legal 'cos there's no such person as John Murphy here. Go back to where you all came from and leave us alone – or it won't be just kicked shins you'll be getting but the taste of lead. Probably like my biscuits!' She laughed out loud.

Jesse could see Joel's split lip and the red weal of a hand print across Kelly's cheek.

'I do so hate bullies,' said Jesse quietly, 'especially to a woman. Come on, you – outside!'

Jesse pushed Frazer in front of him and down the two steps.

'If you want a fight, go ahead, try me instead a slip of a girl like her!' He inclined his head to Kelly, who had followed the others outside.

'There's no need for further violence,' the cowardly Franks piped up. 'You can all stay here and we can work around you.'

'Is that so?' said Jesse.

'Have you been searching for the Bassett

85

gang's hidden loot?' Richards asked the men, rubbing his kicked shin at the same time. Jesse and Joel knew only too well how the man was feeling.

'We have,' said Jesse. 'No luck so far. I guess that's why you're all here.'

'Mr Richards and I are working for the insurance companies that look into bank theft,' Franks explained, an imploring look on his face, hoping that these cowboys and the woman would co-operate. 'If we can recover some of the money then the insurance companies won't have to pay out so much. So you see, we must do our jobs.'

'We can't have people like you finding the money,' Richards added.

Jesse gave a grunt. 'People like us? I don't like the way you said that, mister. We're all hard-working men who earn much more than we're paid. You three wouldn't last five minutes doing the work we do. We don't get no compensation if we break our bones either. So you see, gents, if we dig up some money someone or other buried, then I reckon we're entitled to it,' was Jesse's opinion.

'How about if you all look for it and the ones that find it, keep it,' Kelly suggested.

Jesse smiled. 'Waal, that's a damned fine

idea, Jean. Nothing could be fairer than that.' He turned to the three bank employees. 'That all right by you gents?' he asked.

The three eyed each other and Franks answered for them all.

'It sounds fair to me. But the law says that any money found belongs to the banks.' He noticed Jesse's feet shifting slightly.

'But of course, it all depends on how much we find,' Richards added. 'And you men have the advantage of having looked around already.'

Jesse rubbed his chin thoughtfully. 'True.' He nodded. 'But if you fellers find some freshly dug earth, then you'll know that's where we've already dug, so you've got the advantage of not having to wear yourselves out digging there again.'

All had to agree that what Jesse had just said made perfect sense.

'Have you brought any supplies with you?' Kelly asked the three newcomers.

'We have come prepared,' Frazer told her icily. His look also told her that he had not forgiven her for making him look a fool by knocking his gun out of his hand with the tray of biscuits. Kelly, on the other hand, had not forgiven the man for hitting her and Joel when they had no weapon to defend themselves with.

'In that case,' said Kelly, 'you can prepare your food and we'll prepare ours. We don't aim on feeding you as well as almost being evicted. Pity you took up so much of my time, mister.' She addressed Frazer again. 'We could have had venison stew for supper, now it will take too long to cook to have it tonight.'

Frazer glowered at her and turned to his two charges.

'I'll see to the horses,' he told them, 'and I'll bring in some provisions for us.'

'Very well, Mr Frazer,' Richards replied. He turned to Kelly and whispered something in her ear.

Kelly smiled and pointed to the privy nearly opposite to the cabin.

'I'm afraid it's not very grand, mister, but it serves its purpose.' She giggled.

The others went inside and Kelly started supper for Jesse and his three friends. Joel came up to her.

'Are you okay?' he asked worriedly. Her face had the imprint of Frazer's hand showing vividly now.

Kelly smiled up at him. 'I've suffered worse, Joel. Your lip looks painful. Let me see to it for you,' she offered.

He shook his head. 'I've suffered worse, too. I'm sure glad you got hold of that gun – and that you were wearing your boots!' He grinned.

Kelly turned back to the stove.

'Jean,' he began again, 'it looked as if you knew how to handle a gun. I thought you said you couldn't use one?'

'There are a lot of things you don't know about me, Joel – and best you don't know. Let's leave it at that, shall we?'

Joel nodded and went away to dab at his swollen lip with some water in a bowl on the stoop.

Jesse had been watching the pair conversing. It was obvious that they were on much friendlier terms than the last time he had seen them together. He wondered what exactly had gone on while he and the others were down in the valley that day. He could tell that this young woman was not as scared and timid as she had seemed at first. In fact, she seemed to be an entirely different woman. He would dearly love to get to know her better, but there were too many men around for him to speak to her alone. And after another day, her man would be back.

CHAPTER TEN

After supper and everything was cleared away, the men seemed lost for something to do. There was tension in the air between the two factions: Jesse and his three friends, and Frazer and the two city men. Kelly was glad that Frazer no longer had possession of a gun and was now as helpless as the two he was hired to guard.

Kelly had wanted her gun for protection against Jesse and the rest, but she was certain now that she could trust them and that they would protect her against the three intruders.

Johnny Diamond produced the pack of cards and the four began a poker-game. Frazer and the other two decided to look around outside the cabin, knowing full well that the site had already been checked out by the other faction, and maybe even others before them.

Frazer was unhappy with the outcome of events. With the other four and the girl gone, they would have had a better chance

90

of finding any hidden money. He would have got a bonus if he found anything, besides his payment for taking care of Richards and Franks. Now he felt he was wasting his time.

There would be an hour or two of light left and Kelly decided to take a walk down to the valley and maybe even have a wash in the pool. With so many men around she had had no privacy at all over the past three days. She was sure Jesse would not try and stop her as she had no intention of riding off on one of the horses again.

Frazer noticed her leave with a towel in her hand. He let her go and pretended to be taking care of his two charges. Once Richards and Franks were busy prodding about in the barn, Frazer made some excuse to leave them. He took an indirect route to the valley, to the left of the privy so he would not be seen by anyone looking out of the cabin.

The girl had gone quite some distance in those few minutes. Her walk was quick and graceful with her fiery hair blowing out behind her. Just to look at her made him want to hold her tightly to him. He realized he had not had a woman for quite some time and at that moment he wanted her.

Kelly reached the pool and removed her boots. The water was clear and shallow at the edge where there was fine shingle.

Frazer watched from a distance as she walked in, kicking the water up in front of her like a little girl. Her back was to him and his steps were stealthy and silent. She was unaware of his presence until he grabbed her by the waist and pulled her round to face him.

Kelly's heart lurched within her at the shock. She had not heard him at all.

'Take your hands off me!' Kelly yelled.

'Come on now.' A slight smile crossed his face. 'You're no more married to that red-headed feller than I am. Let's forget what happened before. Just relax and enjoy it, girl.'

His lips came down hard on hers and he held her arms by her side so she was unable to push him away. She no longer wore boots so Frazer knew his shins were safe from her kicks.

It felt good to hold this wriggling woman in his arms. He was much stronger than she and he knew he could subdue her into letting him have his way.

Kelly was by now very afraid. She realized how stupid she had been to leave the safety of Jesse and his men when there was this one around.

Frazer was strong and she felt herself being forced to the ground, but it did not happen. A bullet spat at Frazer's feet and his whole body jumped.

'What the...!'

'Get away from that girl!' It was Jesse's by now familiar slow drawl.

'That's right, attack an unarmed man!' Frazer spat.

'That's right, attack an unarmed woman!' Jesse mimicked.

Kelly ran to Jesse and put her arms around his waist.

'Jesse, I'm so glad you came!' her voice was husky and Jesse could feel her trembling against him.

'Go back to the cabin, Jean!' Jesse told her. 'Me and Mr Frazer here have got something to settle.'

'Leave him, Jesse,' Kelly implored. 'I don't want any killing.'

Jesse released himself from her grip and moved towards Frazer who was looking decidedly pale.

'There are ways of settling things without killing, Jean. Now go on back to the cabin. I wouldn't mind a cup of coffee when I return.'

He smiled at her.

Kelly put her boots back on and reluctantly turned to leave, but she looked back at the two men by the pool. Jesse, she noticed, had returned his gun to its holster. He intended to use fists, she surmised. He was no killer and she was glad.

She could hear the sound of pounding fists on flesh, and grunts. Somehow she could not return to the cabin until she knew Jesse was all right. She knew he could take care of himself but she did not know how fit this other man was. She sat on a rock by the stream which led down to the pool and awaited the outcome.

Ten minutes later she heard a man's footsteps coming towards her. It was surprising how it could get so dark in such a short time. Her heartbeats began to quicken. Which of the two men was coming up the slope towards her? She stood up and peered into the gloom.

When at last she recognized the man as Jesse, her heart seemed to skip a beat. She ran to him and threw her arms around him again.

'Are you hurt, Jesse?' she asked him, looking up at his weather-beaten face which creased into a smile.

'Not as bad as the other feller.' He held her and looked down at her sweet face, only just discernible in the semi-darkness.

'I've grown awful fond of you, Jean,' he told her. 'There's only one more day before your feller gets back and then...' His voice trailed off. 'And then we'll be off,' he finished, but Kelly had a feeling these last words were not the ones he had been thinking.

'You'll like Steve,' she told him. 'He'll be glad you took care of me so well.'

Jesse did not answer, but in the distance there came the rumble of thunder.

'A storm's brewing,' he said. 'I hope it's not gonna be a bad one.'

It felt comforting to feel Jesse's arm around her shoulders as they made their way towards the cabin.

Frazer did not return to the cabin that night and in spite of his behaviour, Kelly started to worry about him when the storm broke and the rain poured down. Had Jesse killed the man? she wondered, or was he so badly injured that he could not make it back to the cabin in time to beat the storm?

Kelly had hidden her gun under the mattress again, but she was sure she would not need it now. She did not fear Richards and Franks, in fact she was sure they feared her more.

The thunderclaps shook the cabin and Kelly would have liked to seek comfort in Jesse's arms, but she dared not go to him with the others there. She would rather have had Steve's arms around her in their bed together. Would he be safe out in this storm? she wondered. He would have already left the town by now and would probably be half-way home. She began to wonder how he would react to all these men being here in the cabin with her. It was almost like being back with the Bassett gang.

Kelly hardly slept at all that night and was glad when it became light. The storm seemed to have abated and it had stopped raining.

There came a knock on the cabin door. At first Kelly thought it must be Steve back home early, but when she lifted up the strong wooden latch that secured the door and opened it, she saw Frazer standing there. His face was cut and had bled during the night. She almost, but not quite, felt sorry for the man.

'Mr Frazer!' Kelly exclaimed. 'Where have you been all night?'

He gave her a dark look. 'In the barn. It weren't too comfortable either!' he spat. He pushed his way in and made for the coffee pot, which was cold.

'Bah!' he growled. 'Not even any coffee!'

'I was just about to make some. Sit down,' she told him. 'You look terrible!'

Kelly suppressed a smile.

Jesse and the others stirred in their bedrolls and were surprised to see Frazer sitting at the table and Kelly making coffee.

'Mornin', Frazer,' said Jesse. 'Did you have a good night?'

Frazer just growled.

Kelly started the breakfast going and realized this was the first meal she had cooked since Steve left. Until now, she had been waited on by the men.

Richards and Franks were eager to start their treasure hunt. They felt they had wasted far too much time already, but when they saw Frazer's face, they wondered if he would be up to any digging.

Jesse knew he and his men would need to make an early start and get out there before the other three. But where would they look? They had covered just about everywhere already.

The stream had risen during the night but

looked as if it was going down now. Jesse decided to follow it right down to the rock pool. Maybe there was some marker they had missed before and the water might reveal it.

Kelly did not want to be left alone in the cabin with the other three and hurried after Jesse and his men.

'I'd like to stay with you four,' Kelly told them. 'I feel much safer with you.'

This seemed to please them all and they felt this morning would be far more enjoyable than the others had been.

Johnny Diamond started digging beneath a large rock they had not noticed before the flood, but they were disappointed when there was no sign of anything like a box or bag.

They were now half-way down the valley and had dug and prodded every so often at the bank of the stream.

Kelly heard voices behind them and turned to see Frazer and his two charges.

'Here they come,' said Kelly, indicating behind her with her thumb.

'Pity you didn't finish that Frazer off last night, Jesse,' said Johnny Diamond.

'I almost thought I had when he didn't come back.' Jesse grinned.

'He daren't show his face,' said Kelly. 'He spent the night in the barn. I bet he was scared out of his pants!'

They all laughed.

The tree that Jesse had investigated the day before, which had been the one that Kelly had used for target practice when Hay Bassett had taught her how to use a gun, looked far different this morning. Lightning had split it in two from top to bottom and some of the bark was burnt.

'Jesse, look!' Kelly pointed. 'I was sure that tree was hollow, and it was!'

She looked behind her and saw that Frazer had noticed the tree also and had started to run towards it.

'Get there first, Jesse!' Kelly ordered. 'You can't let him beat you to it!'

The race to the tree had begun.

CHAPTER ELEVEN

The four cowboys ran towards the tree, but their heeled boots were not made for running, only for getting a firm grip on the stirrups whilst roping steers or broncos, and they looked a comical sight. Frazer, on the other hand, wore conventional boots and in spite of the beating from Jesse the night before, he was making steady progress towards his goal.

Richards and Franks hurried as best they could after him but the man soon left them behind.

Jude was the fleetest of the four friends and reached the tree first, quickly followed by Johnny, Joel, then Jesse.

Jude peered into the charred hollow trunk and they all saw him put his hand inside. He turned, holding up a gunny-sack which, when opened, revealed a slicker which covered the parcel to keep it dry.

By now Frazer had drawn up beside them and when they turned to look at him, he was holding a gun on them all.

'You can hand that over!' he ordered Jude, who looked to Jesse for his decision.

'You agreed that whoever found the money first, would keep it!' Kelly exclaimed in anger.

'Where did you get that gun from, anyhow?' Jesse asked Frazer.

Kelly answered for him. 'It looks as if it might be mine. I hid it under my mattress.'

'Come on, hand it over!' Frazer demanded.

There were four of them, all armed, he realized, and was aware that one of them at least could relieve him of his gun, even if he shot one of them.

With this in mind, he grabbed Kelly's arm and pulled her in front of him, still holding the gun steady in his hand.

'And you can keep your boots to yourself, young woman, do you hear me? One kick out of you and I'll kill you, that's a promise.'

'Good work, Frazer!' Richards smiled, coming forward with his hand out ready to take the sack. 'I'll take that now.'

'The hell you will!' Frazer growled. 'I've got it now and I'm keeping it. Now back off, all of you, or the girl gets it!'

Kelly could feel the man's grip tighten on her arm as he moved away from the group of men.

'Don't be a fool, Frazer!' Franks piped up. 'That's the insurance company's money. You were paid to help us get it and you've done your job. Now hand it over!' Franks held out his hand for the sack.

'I'm not the fool, Franks,' Frazer told the man, 'you two are. The pittance you paid me for bringing you here and taking care of you like babies is an insult. Go back to your company and tell them you couldn't find the money. They'll be none the wiser. Now back off. And one wrong move from any of you, the girl gets it in that pretty little head of hers. I don't know what she is to you men, but I could tell that she means something to you all. You wouldn't want to be the cause of her getting shot, now would you?'

Frazer walked backwards with Kelly shielding him. She knew it would be easy for any of the men to rush Frazer and relieve him of the sack of money, after all, they hardly knew her. Why should they care if she got shot in the process? Money, after all, was worth far more than she was. Maybe she would be able to get away from him at some time. He would need to saddle two horses if he was to take her with him as a shield. He would need two hands for that.

Jesse looked on in exasperation. He was sure it looked as if he and his three friends were cowards, not lifting a finger to save the girl, but he had no intention of doing anything that would jeopardize her life.

'What are we gonna do, Jesse?' Johnny Diamond asked when Frazer and Kelly had got half-way up the incline to the cabin.

'Not much fer the moment,' Jesse answered calmly. 'Let 'em get outa sight, then we'll follow – go round the back of the privy to give us a bit of cover.'

They nodded in agreement, all feeling as helpless as Jesse at that moment.

At last they hurried after Frazer and his prisoner, leaving the two Easterners to their own devices. The two men were in a quandary now that their carer had betrayed them. They followed after the men more slowly, unable to think of what to do next.

Jesse and the others crept behind the privy and peered around the wooden building. Frazer still held a gun on Kelly and was finding it difficult to pull back the pole to the corral and keep an eye on her at the same time. Now he had to catch his horse – and one for Kelly to ride.

'Old American proverb, Mr Frazer,' Kelly called out to him. 'First catch your horse.'

'Bah!' Frazer growled. 'I've never heard of that one.'

Kelly laughed. 'Maybe that's because I just made it up.'

'You don't seem very afraid, miss. You'd do well to feel afraid of me.'

'Mr Frazer, if I had my gun back, you'd feel a darn sight more afraid of me.'

'Get in here and catch the horses!' Frazer demanded.

'I've no idea how to catch a horse, Mr

Frazer,' she smiled at him sweetly. 'I'll tell you what, I'll hold the gun while you catch the horses. How about that?'

Kelly could see the man's face was contorted with fury. He shot off a bullet at her feet, which made her jump back a pace.

'Come on, catch two horses, and be quick about it! The next bullet will go straight through you, that's a promise!'

Kelly could tell he was angry enough to do just that and decided she should obey him now. But she took her time about it.

While Frazer stood and watched Kelly catching the horses with a bridle in her hands ready to place over the animal's head and put the bit in its mouth, Jesse began to creep up behind him, indicating with his hand for the three men to stay put. He was now opposite the cabin and within shooting distance of Frazer.

'Frazer!' Jesse shouted.

Frazer swung round and aimed at Jesse just as Jesse aimed at Frazer. Both bullets were slightly wide of the mark.

'Mr Frazer!' It was Richards who had just reached Jesse, with Franks behind him.

Frazer was distracted for a second and instinctively shot Richards.

Kelly came to the corral opening. Frazer

noticed her out of the corner of his eye and made a grab for the girl, holding her in front of him.

'Now, Jesse, make yourself useful and saddle up two horses. Pronto!'

Jesse was angry with himself at how things had turned out. He was a fool, he told himself, to place himself in such a position as to be of help to Frazer.

The horses were now saddled. Besides Frazer's own horse, Jesse had saddled Richards'. The man would no longer be needing it. And Frazer would now be wanted for murder, he had enough witnesses against him. But now, there was nothing to prevent him from killing the girl whenever he felt like it, for he could only be hanged once, no matter how many he killed.

'Get on that horse, girl!' Frazer ordered.

'Leave her here, Frazer,' Jesse intervened. 'She's expecting a baby and shouldn't be riding. You'd get further away without her slowing you up.'

A smile which looked more like a snarl crossed Frazer's face.

'Don't be such a fool, Jesse! With her with me you won't be following, for if you do, I'll kill her without any qualms. I might even resume where I left off last night by the pool before you came sticking your nose in.' He gave a harsh laugh and motioned with his gun for Kelly to get on the horse.

She mounted up and looked sadly at Jesse, then gave him a small smile.

'Don't worry about me, Jesse,' she said quietly. 'I'm sorry I kicked you – and Joel. Tell Steve I love him when he gets back.'

Jesse nodded and reluctantly let her leave with Frazer.

Joel, Johnny and Jude came hurrying forward. Jude bent down and examined Richards. He sighed.

'I'm sorry about your partner, Mr Franks,' he told the man.

'What's going to happen now?' Franks asked, almost in tears. 'What will the insurance company say when I get back and explain about the money?'

'Damn the money!' Jesse spat. 'I'm more concerned about Jean's safety. I can't just let him take her! I'll give them a start, then I'll follow them at a distance. Maybe I can catch up with them when it gets dark.'

'I'll come with you, Jesse,' Johnny offered.

Jesse shook his head. 'It's best that I go alone. The sound of more than one horse is more likely to reach him at a distance. Look out for Jean's man, Steve. She wants him to know she loves him. Explain things to him carefully – I don't want him gunning for me, too, if he comes after us.'

'Right, Jesse,' Johnny answered.

'And Joel – get that venison stew going! It didn't get cooked when those three jokers turned up. I look forward to some when I get back – with Jean, I hope.'

Joel nodded and gave a small smile. He felt as worried as Jesse about Jean.

Jesse filled his canteen and saddled up, and with a wave, he was off.

Steve had had to shelter underneath the wagon during the storm. He had unhitched the two horses in case they took flight with fear during the storm and left him without transport or his provisions.

He could not wait to get back to Kelly. He hoped she was all right, as he knew she was afraid of storms. He would have loved to have put his arms around her and comforted her while it raged.

Steve was now almost home. Just another couple of hours, he guessed. He smiled at the thought of the greeting he would receive and could not wait to hold her again.

Within a couple of hours Steve could see the familiar outline of the rocks which told him he was practically home. He was soon passing through the entrance to the box canyon which had been Larkinton and two miles further on he came to the narrow ledge leading to Paradise.

Steve halted the horses, dropped the reins to the ground and alighted from the wagon. He would unpack the provisions later, but first he would just take one special parcel wrapped up in brown paper to Kelly. He smiled as he pictured her face when he handed it to her. He hoped she'd like the dress he'd picked out with the help of the woman store-assistant. He had explained that Kelly was expecting a baby and would need a dress that would allow for the expansion of her stomach the nearer her confinement became.

He left the horses and walked across the track. When he had passed between the two boulders and walked a few paces further on, he could see the cabin with smoke coming from the chimney. He hoped she would have something nice for supper as he was feeling hungry.

Then Steve's expression froze. In the corral there were four horses. When he had left four days before there was none. Suddenly he felt alarmed. Was Kelly safe? What could he expect when he reached the cabin? Steve withdrew his gun from its holster as he moved to his left, making his way to the cabin out of direct view from the window. He looked around him. Everywhere was quiet. Too quiet.

CHAPTER TWELVE

He reached the door and gave it a small push with his foot. It swung open and before him, seated at the long table, were four men.

'Keep your hands away from your guns!' Steve ordered the surprised assembly. 'Where's my woman?'

Joel swung his legs over the form and stood up, hands raised.

'You must be Steve,' he said. 'You'd better sit down and we'll explain everything, but I don't think you'll like what you hear. You can put that gun away – we've no intention of attacking you.'

Steve looked at their faces in turn. All except one looked like cowboys. He had been one himself and knew how these men thought and acted and could speak their language. He nodded and replaced his gun, pulling up a chair in the process.

'Come on then, out with it!'

'We arrived here four days ago,' Joel began. 'The place was deserted but we had a feeling it was being occupied. Jesse had the idea a woman lived here as the place was so clean and dust-free.'

'Jean had gone for a swim and when she got back near to the cabin, she saw our horses and was afraid who we might be. She rode off on my horse – to meet up with you, we found out. We didn't know who it was who'd taken it, but Jesse went after the person to get my horse back. He's not so quick-tempered as me.' He allowed a small smile to cross his lips.

'What did you say the woman's name was?' Steve interrupted.

'Said her name was Jean, 'though I reckon she weren't tellin' the truth.'

Steve merely nodded, not agreeing or disagreeing with Joel's assumption, but it was obvious from Steve's question that the girl's name was not Jean.

'Anyhow,' Joel continued, 'Jesse brought her back here. We done her no harm, Steve, believe me.' He grinned, 'In fact, she did Jesse and me more harm by kicking our shins a couple o' times! She's quite a gal!'

'Which one of you is Jesse?' Steve asked him.

'He's not here,' he said. 'I'll tell you what happened.' And Joel proceeded to tell Steve everything that had happened since they had arrived at the cabin.

'Jesse and the rest of us found the loot, hidden in a hollow tree. We missed it before but lightning struck the tree in the storm and split it in two. Frazer, Richards and Franks, here,' he pointed to the insurance man, 'came up at the same time and Frazer grabbed Jean and used her as a shield to escape with her and the loot. He threatened that anyone who followed would be shot, and so would the girl.'

Steve's lips were pursed into a thin line.

'Why the hell was he allowed to keep his gun?' He almost shouted in annoyance and disbelief.'

'He wasn't,' Joel insisted. 'Seems he found Jean's gun which she'd hidden under the mattress.'

Steve was thinking it over, picturing in his mind everything that Joel had described.

'There is one thing I omitted,' said Joel. 'Well, two things actually.'

'Oh, and what're they?' asked Steve.

'The day this Frazer feller arrived – he punched me on the lip...' Joel hesitated in finishing his sentence, 'and he slapped Jean hard across her face, knocking her to the floor. That was before she turned the tables on him. Also,' he added, watching Steve's face intently, 'he followed Jean down to the pool that evening and tried it on with her. Jesse saved her just in time.'

Steve's face was as black as thunder at all Kelly had gone through while he'd been away.

'Come on, finish the story!' Steve prompted impatiently. 'Where's Kelly, this Frazer feller, and Jesse?'

'Oh, so her name's Kelly, is it?' Joel smiled.

Steve could have kicked himself for revealing her real name, which Kelly had obviously wanted kept from these men.

'Here you are, Steve.' It was Jude interrupting. 'Have a cup of coffee. You look as if you can use one.'

Steve took it from the man. It was odd being offered a cup of coffee from a stranger in his own home.

'Where is Kelly now – and Jesse and Frazer?' Steve asked.

'We followed at a distance and Frazer tried

112

to get Jean – Kelly – to catch two horses and saddle them. Richards said something and Frazer wasn't expecting him to be there just then and he just shot the man. Jesse had crept up closer while this was going on but Frazer saw him. He could have shot him there and then but he needed him to saddle the horses as I don't think the girl could manage it. After that he warned that if anyone followed, he'd shoot her.' Joel sighed slightly. 'So you see, Jesse couldn't follow them straight away. We all wanted to go with Jesse, but he said one horse wouldn't be heard as much as several.'

'Well, I'm going after them. I can't just sit here and leave it to this Jesse.'

'OK,' said Joel, 'but if anyone can rescue her, Jesse can. I'll come with you.'

'Get some food down you first, Steve,' Johnny Diamond advised. 'You'll do a lot better on a full stomach than an empty one. It's venison stew. Joel here cooked it and it's pretty good even though he's no cook.'

Steve thought it over for a second or two and had to admit that Johnny was right. He tucked into a plateful.

'I'll come along too, Steve,' Johnny offered.

'And me,' added Jude.

'What about this joker?' Joel jerked his thumb at the insurance man. 'Jesse said fer someone to watch him.'

'I didn't see anyone on my way here,' said Steve. 'I reckon they went in the direction of Hazelworth.'

Johnny Diamond frowned. 'I reckon that's where Frazer's headed. He won't want to take Jean – Kelly – into town or she'll spill the beans to the sheriff about what went on up here and that he shot Richards.'

Steve met his violet eyes and their gaze held there for a few seconds.

'You're hinting that Frazer will either kill Kelly or leave her behind before he reaches Hazelworth?'

'I guess I am,' Johnny replied.

'Kelly wouldn't go to Hazelworth in any case.'

'How's that?' asked Joel.

Steve did not answer. He feared he had said too much already by telling the men Kelly's real name. This insurance man would probably put two and two together and realize that Kelly was the same woman who had supposedly gone down a ravine with Tobin and the prison-wagon guards.

'I'm leaving now,' said Steve. 'If you want to come along, then let's go!'

114

'Are we bringing Franks here along too, or shall we leave him behind?' asked Jude.

'Bring him,' Joel told him. 'We'll escort him to Hazelworth and put him on a train east.'

All the men left the cabin and made their way to the corral where they saddled up and moved out. Franks was between the men and the crossing for him was no easier this time.

'Shut your eyes, Mr Franks,' Johnny advised, knowing how afraid the man was. 'We'll tell you when you've reached the other side.'

Franks did as he was told and let out a sigh of relief when he realized that he had reached flat, grassy ground.

As they rode, Steve got to know his companions. They were an easy-going bunch and he felt at home in their company. He had missed the ranch work he had been used to since he had been banished from the Johnson spread after Quincy and Hankins had beaten him up so badly. He smiled as he recalled the short time he had worked in the Hazelworth restaurant with the owner Sarah Dobson, and also his time with Kelly while she awaited her trial. He shook his head wistfully. It seemed as if he would never be settled with her. There always seemed to be something that came between them to keep them apart. Now he was really afraid for her safety. From what he'd heard about Frazer, Kelly could be in real danger. He had killed Richards, the other insurance man, so it would not worry him at all if he killed Kelly also.

All too soon it became dark and the men knew they would have to dismount and rest up until dawn, but Steve had other ideas.

'I don't care what you men are doing, but I'm going on. You're all cowboys and you know that cowboys can see in the dark.'

The men gave a short laugh.

'Yeah, mebbe you're right, Steve,' said Joel. 'But we'd better take it slow, we don't want our mounts to tread in a gopher hole or something. We'll have to watch our direction too. We don't want to end up going round in circles.'

'Just follow your nose,' Steve told them.

They rode all night and at first light they could see a stationary horse, its reins hanging straight down.

'I'm sure that's Jesse's grey gelding.' Johnny Diamond spoke out. 'But where's Jesse?'

CHAPTER THIRTEEN

As Kelly moved out of the corral on Richards' horse her eyes met Jesse's. She could tell he was afraid for her safety and that he felt so helpless with Frazer pointing a gun at her. She gave him a smile to try and reassure him that she would be all right. She caught sight of the others in the background, all looking on, equally helpless. She rode past the dead body of Richards. She did not feel that much sorrow over his death, but because of it, she knew what Frazer was capable of. There was no doubt that once she had served her purpose by keeping Jesse and the others off his back, he would not hesitate to kill her.

She reached the two boulders and passed between them. As she started over the narrow track her thoughts were of Steve. Would she ever see him again? she wondered sadly. There always seemed to be someone, something, to keep them apart. Would they ever be left in peace to continue their life together and be happy?

'Keep back!' Frazer ordered Jesse as he stepped forward before Frazer went past the two boulders. 'Remember, if you shoot me in the back, the reflexes in my fingers can still pull the trigger and the girl gets it. I have a feeling that you don't want that to happen. Now walk away – now!'

Jesse sighed and did as the man ordered. But he silently vowed he would get the man, no matter how long it took.

Kelly was forced to ride in front of Frazer and she could almost feel the presence of his gun pointed at her back.

'Get a move on, girl!' he shouted at her.

Kelly urged her mount on, but she had no intention of making the animal gallop. For one thing she did not want to get too far away from the men in Paradise, and for another, she had her baby's welfare to think of.

She realized at that moment how dependent she had become on her gun, which she had worn on her hip for over three months while with the Bassett gang, and when she escaped from the prison wagon with Jim and Hankins. She knew she had become hardened over that time and had lost part of her femininity. Steve had noticed that when he and US Marshal Luke Dalton came up to them on the trail whilst they were still asleep. Being able to use a gun so proficiently had made Steve alter his feelings for her while he had lost his memory.

Her thoughts went to Jim Tobin. He had insisted she wear a dress once they reached Paradise and that she put away her gun for good. Poor Jim. He had not lived to see her in a dress. She had kept her word about the gun as well. But then, Kelly had to admit, she had not had cause to use one until now, and now she did not have one to use.

Frazer forced Kelly to ride until dusk fell. She felt exhausted as she dismounted, almost collapsing with fatigue.

The spot where they had stopped seemed to be in a depression and Frazer knew they would not be spotted so easily from a distance.

Kelly made no attempt to unsaddle her horse. She sat on the ground and watched Frazer put one of the saddles down and the other about five feet away.

'Take your boots off!' he ordered. 'You're not going to kick me like you did Richards.'

Kelly reluctantly obeyed.

Frazer placed one of the bedrolls next to a saddle, then the other next to the first.

'Now your dress!'

She looked at him aghast.

'I will not!' Kelly declared.

'You can either take it off by yourself...' he hesitated ominously, 'or I'll rip it off you. Which is it to be, girl?'

Kelly stood up and hung her head. After a few seconds she slowly began to take her dress off.

'That's better!' He gave her a smile, or rather a leer.

He pulled her to him and she could feel his breath over her neck. His hands gripped her arms as his lips came down on to hers. Kelly tried to pull away, but he was determined.

'Are you going to co-operate with me?' he asked her.

'No I'm not!' she told him. 'If you do anything to me ... I'll kill you!'

Frazer laughed out loud. 'Now how in hell are you gonna do that?'

'I don't know yet. But I will,' she declared.

'Get on that bedroll!' he ordered, and fetched a rope from his own saddle.

Kelly stood her ground. She was not going to give up before a fight, although she knew she would come off worse.

Frazer wrapped one end of the rope around her wrists, tying it tightly. The rough hemp cut into her flesh and it felt sore. The man gave her a shove and she fell on to the bedroll. The next second he was down beside her. He pulled her arms up above her head and tied the rope around the saddle. She knew that in this position, she would not be able to move her arms because of the weight of the saddle. With the other end of the rope he tied her ankles and attached it to the other saddle, making her unable to lift her feet.

Tears began to form in Kelly's eyes. Her heart was beating abnormally fast and she felt very afraid – and angry.

'You're a coward, Mr Frazer,' she told him. 'A low-down yellow coward! Have you no shame – no pity?'

'You're like most women – you talk too much. Now shut up!'

Jesse allowed Kelly and Frazer to become almost a speck in the distance before he followed. He was angry with himself for allowing this to happen. He had given Jean, as he knew her, his word that he would keep her safe, yet now she was in deadly danger. He knew that if he had been a hard man what had happened would never have occurred, but he was not. His only thoughts were for Jean's safety and nothing else.

He rode steadily, not getting too close to the pair. He knew they would have to stop when it got dark. Then, he hoped, would be his chance to rescue her. But would he be in time? What terrible ordeal would Jean have had to go through before he could carry out a rescue attempt?

Jesse, despite trying to deny the fact to himself, was now completely under Jean's spell. Her beautiful face, surrounded by all that fiery hair, was superimposed in his mind. If only she was not some other man's woman. If only she was his. But Jesse was under no illusions. He was forty-three years old, a cowboy and bronc-buster, and if he did not get that money back from Frazer, he had nothing to offer any woman. He hadn't even got youth and good looks on his side to make a woman want him for a husband.

The thought of Jean consumed him during the whole journey. Strangely the stolen money now in Frazer's possession was not as important as it had been at the start. All those plans he had made for what he would do with it when he found it, had been forgotten.

With his mind so preoccupied it surprised him how quickly dusk fell. He wondered how far ahead of him the two were. He decided to keep riding in the same direction until he came upon them.

Jesse dismounted. He was at the top of a gradual downward slope and as his eyes had already become accustomed to the darkness, he could see the two he had been following a short distance away below him. He took hold of his mount's reins and led it away some distance from the spot. He foot-hobbled the animal with his bandanna and placed a hand over its velvety nose, a signal to it to keep quiet. Taking the coiled lariat in his hands, he moved forward again quietly. He lay on his stomach and peered over the edge. Jesse's heart dropped as he saw Frazer with Jean. It looked as if he had tied her down, hands and feet. His teeth ground in anger.

He moved silently, slowly, towards the pair on the ground. Jesse's hands played out the rope and as Frazer pulled up from Jean, he whirled it around a couple of times above his head. It travelled at speed, to fall deftly over Frazer's shoulders.

Jesse hurried forward, playing in the rope as he did so. When he reached the man he wound the coils around his body, securing his arms to his sides. Frazer was now in no position to do any more harm.

While he was so secured, Jesse could not resist the urge to give the man a terrific punch on the nose, which flattened him.

Jesse knelt down on one knee beside Jean's almost naked body.

'Jean ... oh Jean ... I'm so sorry!' he whispered as he began to untie the ropes that bound her.

'You were just a little bit too late this time, Jesse.' Her voice was husky, almost inaudible.

There were tears in Jesse's eyes as he pulled her clothes over her body. He looked around for her dress and found it nearby and helped her on with it.

Kelly allowed herself to be lifted up and she felt safe and secure in the tall man's arms. She could feel his body shaking against her and knew that he was shedding silent tears for her.

'I love you so much, Jean,' he whispered to her. 'I've let you down badly. I can't expect you to forgive me.'

Her arms held him tighter to her, her ear was over his rapidly beating heart.

'There was nothing you could have done, Jesse,' she told him. 'You're here now.'

Four riders sat their mounts at the top of the rise and looked down at the scene.

Steve's teeth ground in anger at seeing Kelly in another man's arms. By the way she was holding on to him it seemed as if he meant an awful lot to her. Which he did.

CHAPTER FOURTEEN

'Is that feller with Kelly, Jesse or Frazer?' Steve asked of them all.

Johnny answered: 'It's Jesse.'

'Steve, it ain't what it looks like,' said Joel.

'And what *does* it look like to you, Joel?'

The man gave a small cough. 'Whatever – it ain't.'

Steve moved off down the slope. Kelly and Jesse released themselves from each other's arms.

'Steve!' Kelly cried with pleasure. 'It's you!'

He dismounted and they ran to each other. As Kelly came into his arms, Steve looked at Jesse, who stood nearby. He also noticed another man trussed up on the ground.

'That must be Frazer,' he observed to Jesse.

Jesse nodded and turned away. The moment with Jean in his arms had been

125

good while it lasted. Now she would only have eyes for Steve.

'Oh, Steve.' Kelly held him close. 'It's been terrible. I wish I'd gone with you to fetch provisions in the wagon. Those bumps along the way would have been nothing to what I've been through.'

'What did Frazer do to you, Kelly?' Steve asked her, fearing the answer.

'His worst,' was her reply, and Steve noticed the catch in her voice.

'I'm gonna kill him!' Steve shouted and moved towards Frazer's supine body.

The company all looked towards the two and felt slightly uncomfortable. They felt in part to blame for what had happened to Kelly by not protecting her from Frazer.

'Steve!' Kelly shouted after him. 'Leave it to the law. He'll be tried for murder. No one would be interested in what he did to me. After all, you know where I am supposed to be now.'

The men frowned and looked at each other for an explanation of Kelly's words, but Steve knew they would never get one.

'I did tell him I'd kill him if he did anything to me,' said Kelly. 'But I'll take my revenge in another way.' She moved towards Frazer who was looking up at them, fear in

126

his eyes.

'Untie him, Jesse,' Kelly ordered.

'Best he stays tied, Jean,' was Jesse's opinion.

'Do as I say, please,' she insisted.

Jesse unwound the rope that bound Frazer tightly and the men moved around him in a circle so he would not be able to escape.

Kelly walked up to the man, who remained on the ground.

'Stand up, Mr Frazer!' Kelly ordered.

Frazer got to his feet, looking around him at the men whose faces were stern and angry.

'Take off your boots!' was Kelly's next order.

Reluctantly Frazer did so, nearly overbalancing in the process.

'Now take your pants off.'

Some of the men grinned at this, others looked rather alarmed.

Frazer hesitated at this request. His belt was already unbuckled as he had not had time to buckle it when Jesse had thrown a rope around him. At last he pulled his pants down.

'That's right,' said Kelly. 'Now your shirt and longjohns.'

'No, I won't do that!' Frazer exclaimed in alarm.

'What was that?' asked Kelly. 'I didn't quite hear what you said.' She cupped her hand to her ear and cocked her head on one side.

'I said I won't take my shirt and longjohns off.'

'Oh,' said Kelly, sounding slightly disappointed. 'What was it you said to me when I told you I wouldn't take my dress off?'

He did not answer.

'Come on now, what did you say?' she insisted.

'I said I'd rip it off you,' he mumbled.

'Sorry, I must be going deaf. What did you say you'd do?'

Frazer breathed heavily and looked around him for a possible escape, knowing full well there wasn't one.

'I said I'd rip it off you,' he said a little louder.

'Yes, that was it.' Kelly gave him a beaming smile. 'Now are you going to take your shirt and longjohns off, or would you like me to rip them off you?'

Frazer started unbuttoning his shirt and took it off slowly. Then gradually, very reluctantly, he pulled off his longjohns.

'Jean, you didn't ought to see him like this.' Jesse came forward.

'No, and he had no right seeing me like

that either!'

She had had her revenge, but it did not feel good. She turned to Steve, buried her head in his chest and cried.

'Take me home, Steve,' she whispered.

Johnny Diamond came up with the gunny-sack taken from the lightning tree.

'I don't like mentioning it at a time like this,' he began, 'but what'll we do with this?'

Franks pushed his way forward, eyes widening.

'You know full well what must be done with it,' he said. 'That money belongs to the banks. Now, gentlemen, hand it over and nothing will happen to you. If you don't...' Franks looked at them all, trying to sound brave and important, but inside his stomach was churning with nerves, 'then the law will take proceedings and you could all be in big trouble.'

'What shall we do, Jesse?' Johnny asked him.

Jesse was unsure. If this man Franks here, and Richards and Frazer hadn't turned up when they did, then the money would by now have been distributed among the four of them and their lives would have been changed. But Jesse, for his part, knew that his life had already been changed.

'I guess all four of us will be on the run from the law if we don't hand it over,' he reasoned.

'I'm willing to take my chances on that,' said Joel.

Kelly moved out of Steve's arms and turned to the men.

'What if you give some of it back to Mr Franks, then maybe he will let you keep the rest as a reward for finding it?' she suggested hopefully.

'Yeah,' said Joel. 'How about it, Mr Franks?'

'Well, I don't know...' he spluttered, his eyes moving quickly from one face to another. 'Perhaps we'd better count it first, just to see how much there is.'

'Good idea,' said Jude, and everyone looked at him and grinned. It wasn't often Jude said anything.

The gunny-sack was opened and the almost new Fish slicker was spread out on the ground. There were five bundles of bank-notes. Franks gave one each to Jesse, Joel, Johnny and Jude and kept the fifth for himself to count.

'Are you sure you can count more than ten?' Joel ribbed Johnny.

'I can use my fingers and toes to count on

more than once,' he answered good-humouredly.

Kelly and Steve stood by and watched the men counting out the money. There looked to be quite a lot, but then Hay Bassett had robbed a lot of banks over the years. Also Larkinton had been his town and he had received all the profits from the businesses – the hotel, restaurant, general store and the gaming-tables.

After one or two recounts, they came up with a grand total of just over $100,000.

'How much do we get for finding it then, Mr Franks?' Johnny Diamond asked him.

Franks thought it over for a few seconds. 'How about five per cent each?' he asked.

The men scratched their heads. Figuring wasn't exactly their strong point.

'What does that make it – each?' asked Joel.

'Five thousand dollars,' replied Franks. 'That would leave eighty thousand for the banks.'

'It sounds fair enough,' said Jesse. 'Shall we shake on it?' He looked around at his men. They all nodded in agreement.

'Hold on a minute,' Joel interjected. 'What about Jean – Kelly? She was with us when we found the money, and she lives on the land. Shouldn't she get a cut?'

Kelly answered right away. 'No thanks. It's blood-money. I don't want anything to do with it.'

They all looked at her with frowns on their faces.

'You sure, Jean?' Jesse asked her.

'Quite sure, Jesse.'

Franks's face was a picture of glee.

'Very commendable of you, young lady.' He was glad he would not have to make another split in the reward.

'Right, Mr Franks. It's a deal.' Jesse nodded. 'We'll take five thousand dollars each, and thank you very much.'

'Just as long as he don't run off with it for himself, like Frazer here did,' Joel put forward.

'I can assure you, Joel, that I'm an honourable man and the eighty thousand dollars will be placed in my company's hands.'

'OK.' Joel grinned. 'We believe you.'

Kelly took Steve to one side away from the others' hearing.

'Steve, what if Franks tells people about me? He knows my name's Kelly now and someone might remember it from newspaper reports or even from the actual trial?'

'We might even get the law up in Paradise

to fetch Richards' body. Sheriff Todd even.'

Kelly felt shaky at the thought. Sheriff Todd knew who she was as she had spent a short time in his jail while the trial of Jim Tobin, Hankins and herself took place. He had watched her go off in the prison wagon and had been informed by US Marshal Luke Dalton that she was now dead.

'Steve, we daren't stay in Paradise any longer. We must hurry back quickly, get the legacy that Doc Reynolds left me and go somewhere new.'

Steve held her close. 'You're right, Kelly, I'm sorry to say. It's a real shame we've got to leave our home, but maybe it's for the best. We'll find somewhere near to a doctor for when the baby comes.'

Frazer still stood there minus his clothes, his hands placed in a strategic position.

'Give me back my clothes!' he shouted as he felt sure everyone had forgotten him.

'What shall we do with him, Jean?' Jesse asked her. 'It's up to you to decide, after what he did to you.'

'You'll be taking him in to Hazelworth, won't you?' she asked.

Franks intervened. 'Yes, we'll let the law deal with him. He'll get a fair trial, but we all know what the verdict will be.'

'It might sound kinda vindictive,' Kelly began, 'but I'd like him to have to walk all the way – dressed just the way he is.'

Everyone laughed, for he was not dressed at all.

'OK, that's a fair enough sentence.' Joel grinned. 'Are you coming with us to Hazelworth, Kelly?'

Kelly shook her head. 'No. All of you go on without us. Steve and me – well, we've got some catching up to do and we'd like to have the cabin to ourselves for a few days. You're all welcome to return and overwinter there if you like. But maybe you won't need to with so much money between you now.'

'We'll think about it,' said Jesse. 'I've a feeling this is goodbye, Jean – or rather, Kelly.'

'Think of me as Jean,' she said. 'It's been nice meeting you all. Take care now, and don't spend all that money too quickly.'

Jesse stepped forward. He gave a quick look at Steve before bending his head and kissing Kelly gently on the mouth.

'You take care, too, Jean. I won't ever forget you.'

Kelly smiled up at him, tears forming in her eyes.

'Nor me you, Jesse. Goodbye. Don't forget,

134

you can stay in the cabin if you want to.'

The four cowboys and Franks mounted up, but Frazer was left to walk beside the horses. Kelly and Steve gave them a wave, mounted their own horses and headed back to Paradise.

'I've a feeling you wanted Frazer to walk all the way to Hazelworth because it would take longer.' Steve smiled across at her as they rode.

'You've learnt to read my mind,' she smiled back. 'It'll give us more time to get to Paradise and leave again before anyone comes.'

'Are you all right, Kelly?' he asked in concern. 'I mean – after what happened to you?'

She nodded. 'I just want to forget it, Steve. I want to start afresh.'

Steve looked behind him and could see the men riding slowly with Frazer stumbling along. How his feet must hurt, Steve mused. But serve him right! was his verdict.

CHAPTER FIFTEEN

Johnny Diamond was riding alongside Jesse on their way to Hazelworth. He took occasional glances across at his friend and knew something was wrong. He had not spoken for an hour and his face was expressionless. Johnny had the feeling that Jesse's thoughts were still with the girl he had left with Steve. He guessed that Jesse had fallen for her in a big way. It was understandable as she had affected them all to some degree.

'Are we going back to Paradise later, Jesse?' Johnny ventured to ask at last.

'I doubt it,' Jesse replied.

'Kelly said we'd be welcome,' Johnny reminded him.

'Jean,' Jesse insisted. 'Her name's Jean.'

Johnny shook his head. 'That's not what Steve called her, and he should know.'

'Her name's Jean,' Jesse repeated. 'She said she wanted us to think of her as Jean. I don't want you to talk of her as Kelly – do you understand?' He rose slightly in the saddle and looked around him. 'Listen,' he said, 'the girl's name is Jean. No one is to call her Kelly. If anyone does...' he hesitated, 'I'll punch you one. Do you all hear me? Mr Franks – are you listening?'

Franks seemed to shrivel up in the saddle at Jesse's booming voice.

'Yes – yes of course, Jesse. Her name's Jean.'

'Right,' Jesse said and his look was met by the others' surprised expressions.

Four hours later they could see the town of Hazelworth in the distance.

'I suppose we'd better let Frazer put his clothes back on before we reach town,' Joel said reluctantly.

'I suppose we had,' said Jesse glumly.

'He's almost had it,' said Joel.

'He's got that to come,' Jesse grunted. 'After what he did to Jean, I've got no sympathy for the man – though he's not even a man! He even had to tie her hand and foot or she'da made it hard on him, that's fer sure!'

Johnny knew the thought of what had happened was eating Jesse up and it hurt him to see his friend so despondent.

Joel stopped beside Frazer and threw his boots and clothes down to him.

'Here you are, Mr Frazer. You'd better

137

look a bit respectable before we reach town. We don't want you to frighten all the ladies now, do we? I sure hope you're able to get your boots on again. Your feet look a bit swollen to me. Shame, that!'

The men laughed quietly and watched while Frazer donned his clothes. He had a lot of difficulty pulling on his boots, but no one offered to help him.

'I'll come in with you to the sheriff, Mr Franks,' Jesse told him. 'We must get everything straight, mustn't we? We can't have you forgetting exactly what happened up there in Paradise, can we?'

Franks looked uneasy. Jesse's slow, quiet manner was deceiving. There was a air of menace in his tone which made Franks begin to tremble.

'Of course, Jesse,' he answered.

They rode down the street and onlookers stopped to stare at seeing one man walking beside the horses. He was hobbling and he was wearing a noose around his neck, the other end held by Jesse.

They stopped outside the sheriff's office. Jesse dismounted first.

'You others go and get yourselves a drink – but don't go getting drunk and shooting your mouths off, you hear me?'

The three nodded as if taking orders from their father.

'I'll meet you in there when we've had a little chat with the sheriff. Come on, Mr Franks, down you get!'

Franks dismounted unsteadily and Jesse caught his elbow to support him when he'd reached the ground. The small man looked up at his tall helper and squeezed a smile from his face in thanks.

Jesse gave Frazer a light push in his back to encourage him up the two steps to the boardwalk.

'In you go, Frazer!' Jesse ordered.

Frazer was in no condition to object or to try and escape and almost fell through the door of Sheriff Daniel Todd's office.

Todd had his feet on his desk and was reading the *Weekly Clarion* when they entered. He looked up from the paper and removed his boots from his desk.

'What have we got here?' he asked, his eyes going from one to the other of the three men who stood before him.

'My name's Jesse Cahill,' Jesse announced. 'This here's Mr Franks from an insurance company back East, and this other specimen is Mr Frazer, formerly in the employ of said insurance company.'

'What's' – the sheriff pointed to Frazer – 'he doing with a noose round his neck?'

'I put it there,' said Jesse. 'I thought he ought to get the feeling of what it'll be like when it happens for real. He shot a Mr Richards, colleague of Mr Franks up in a place called Paradise. Mebbe you've heard of it?'

Todd stood up. The expression on his face was difficult to fathom but the word 'Paradise' had certainly hit the spot.

'Paradise!' he breathed. 'Well, I sure have heard of it! It used to be the Bassett gang's hideout.'

'Me and my three friends read all about it in a newspaper and decided to give the place a visit,' Jesse went on. 'We planned on overwintering in the cabin there and at the same time, search for the gang's hidden loot.'

'Did you find it?' Todd asked with interest.

'Sure did!' said Jesse. 'The trouble was, this here Frazer feller was paid to escort the two men up there. They worked for the insurance company working for the banks that the gang had robbed. They intended finding the money so they wouldn't have to pay the banks so much.'

Todd nodded his understanding of the matter.

'Waal,' Jesse drawled, 'me and my friends found it just before Frazer, Richards and Franks came up. There was a young woman living in the cabin and she was with us when we found the loot. Frazer grabbed the girl as a shield and made us hand over the money. He took her with him and we all went after him at a distance so he didn't shoot her, and Franks and Richards came up on him from a different direction and when Richards spoke to him, Frazer shot him down in cold blood. He then took off with the woman as a hostage so we wouldn't follow him. But we did.'

'What happened to the woman?' Todd asked.

Jesse ground his teeth. 'He did the lowest thing a man could do to a woman. And he tied her hand and foot before he done it!'

The dark scowl on Jesse's face as he looked at Frazer was terrible to see and the man whose nose had obviously been punched by the look of the dried blood around it, was glad at that moment that he was under the protection of the law and not let loose on Jesse.

'Where's the woman now?' Todd asked.

Jesse hesitated a fraction of a second before answering:

'She's gone back up to Paradise with her man.'

'Where did he appear from?' Todd was beginning to become a bit confused.

'He'd been off to get supplies for winter and returned after she'd been taken off by Frazer. He came along with the others after I'd gone on ahead.'

'I'd better have their names for the record,' said Todd, pulling over a piece of paper and a pencil.

'Her name's Jean and his is Steve.'

'Her name's Kelly,' Frazer said maliciously. He had no idea what the implications were, but he knew she had used a false name to them at the beginning. She must have had her reasons, but everyone guessed that she did not want anyone to know her real name.

'What!' Todd exclaimed, his face a picture of surprise and disbelief. 'That's not at all a common name. There was a Kelly once who went down a ravine inside a prison wagon. She was tried in this very town. She used to be Hay Bassett's woman. It seems a mighty big coincidence that another Kelly is living up there in Paradise – and with a man called Steve.'

'What are you saying, Sheriff?' Franks interposed. 'Could that Kelly who went down a ravine and this one be one and the same?'

Todd stroked his chin thoughtfully. He shook his head.

'No, it couldn't be. It was US Marshal Luke Dalton who gave us the information. He wouldn't lie. Why would he?'

'This Steve,' Jesse began slowly, 'how does he fit in the picture? Was he wanted by the law?'

Todd shook his head. 'No, he was one of the posse who went to Larkinton and up to Paradise. He rescued Kelly from Bassett who'd kept her prisoner – although they got pretty pally up there by all accounts.'

Jesse felt a cold tingle run down his back. Todd was discussing Jean, the woman who had reached him as no other woman had since his wife had died many years before. If Jean – or Kelly as Steve called her – *was* this Kelly Todd was telling them about, then it was no wonder that she did not want anyone to know her real name. Jesse realized that he did not really know her at all.

'How long had this Kelly known Steve?' Jesse ventured to ask.

'Before she got in with the Bassett gang,' said Todd. 'It appears he had been looking for her after she was taken off by the gang and her stepfather. He worked in the restaurant to make enough money to get himself up to Wyoming, where he thought she'd gone. The girl escaped from the gang once, but they brought her back again, but while she was free for a while, she got word to the law where the gang hid out.'

Todd frowned darkly. 'I just can't make out why Dalton said she was dead when it seems like she ain't.'

Jesse could. Jean – or Kelly – had escaped from the wagon somehow before it went over the ravine, and she was now up in Paradise with Steve!

CHAPTER SIXTEEN

'Where's this Marshal Dalton now?' asked Jesse.

'Left town. Got married to Sarah Dobson who ran the restaurant and they went East somewhere.'

Smart move, Jesse thought to himself. He wondered why the man had lied about Jean being dead. Could he have fallen under her spell as he himself had? He would not have

144

been at all surprised if this was the case.

Todd took the keys to the cells from his desk drawer and motioned to Frazer to go before him.

'You don't walk too well, Mr Frazer,' the sheriff remarked.

'Ask him why!' Frazer growled.

'Oh, I don't think I'll bother,' Todd said. 'I'm sure Mr Cahill had his reasons to make you hobble. Now get in there and if you behave yourself, my deputy'll bring you some supper.'

Jesse had perched himself on the corner of the sheriff's desk awaiting the lawman's return to his office.

'What happens now?' Jesse asked him.

'What happened to Richards' body – is it still up there in Paradise?' Todd asked.

Franks answered as he had still been there after Jesse had gone after Frazer and Kelly.

'His body was put in the barn with a tarpaulin over him. For all I know, he's still there. Will you be sending anyone up there to fetch him?'

'Yeah, I'll probably have to go up there myself. I'll take a look at this Kelly and Steve. They could hardly be anyone else but the ones I know. Steve Culley was Hay Bassett's son – did you know that?'

This came as a shock to Jesse and it showed plainly on his face.

'I don't understand,' said Jesse. 'If Steve Culley was Hay Bassett's son, why did he join the posse who went after him?'

Todd shrugged his shoulders. 'Seems like Culley hadn't seen his pa for years. Hay Bassett had walked out on him and his ma and they hadn't heard from him since. He took on the surname of the man his ma married. Hay Bassett didn't recognize him when they came face to face. It was Culley who shot Hay Bassett.'

Jesse was quiet. His face looked thoughtful as he was picturing the scene up there in Paradise, and he wondered how all this had affected Jean.

'When will you be going up to Paradise, Sheriff?' Jesse asked the lawman.

'Tomorrow I guess. If there's only the two of them up there we shouldn't need a posse, just a couple of men will do.'

Jesse stood up from his perch on the corner of the sheriff's desk.

'If this Steve and Kelly are the same ones ... will you be arresting them?'

Todd sat down in his chair again.

'Of course! Kelly was sentenced to ten years' imprisonment for riding with the

146

Bassett gang. She took part in a bank hold-up in this very town. One of the bank tellers was shot. She'll have to go to prison and serve her sentence. I don't think she should have been given so long, mind you,' was his opinion. 'She did, after all, let the law know where the gang's hideout was. It was a well-kept secret until then. But it's not my job to question the judge's decision. Steve will have to be arrested for aiding and abetting a felon to escape.'

Jesse understood now why Jean had refused a cut of the stolen money. She said it was 'blood money', and she should know, having been one of the raiders on the bank where the teller had been shot. He felt in a quandary now. He knew he must go back to Paradise and warn them to leave quickly before the sheriff arrived to arrest them both. But would he get there in time? Even if he did, should he warn them, for he, too would then be wanted for tipping them off.

Why was he even questioning his decision to go back to Paradise? He *had* to warn Jean – and Steve of course.

'You won't be needing me any more now, will you, Sheriff?' Jesse asked.

'Not until later. You'll be sticking around though, won't you?'

'I dare say,' was Jesse's reply. 'Coming, Mr Franks?'

Jesse did not give the little man time to answer as he was propelled out of the sheriff's office.

'You'll need a room for the night,' said Jesse. 'The hotel's up the street a ways. Will you be leaving in the morning?'

'I must get back and place this money with my company,' Franks replied.

'Yes, you do that. You don't want anyone stealing it from you, do you? Goodbye now!' Jesse tipped his hat to the man and went to the saloon.

His three friends had got into a card-game with another man when Jesse walked up to them. Jesse beckoned Joel over out of earshot. Joel reluctantly left his hand face down on the table and came up to his friend.

'What's wrong, Jesse? You look as if you've had some bad news.' Joel smiled.

'I have, Joel. I'm not sure what to do. Can you cut short the game and come outside? I don't want anyone else overhearing.'

Joel's face now looked as worried as Jesse's.

'Sure, Jesse. I'll tell the others. We'll be out soon. I've been dealt a rotten hand anyhow.'

Jesse did not often smoke, but now

seemed to be the right occasion. He took out his small leather bag of Bull Durham from his shirt pocket and opened it up. He then produced some papers, took one and then placed some of the tobacco evenly along the middle of its length. He rolled it up, licked one side and sealed it. From a small pocket at the front of his trousers he took a match and flicked it alight with his thumbnail. Each process was performed as if in slow motion, and the smoke was inhaled as if it was needed as a drug to help him think.

He knew he had to get to Paradise fast. He must be there before the sheriff and a couple of men arrived so that he could give Jean and Steve time to get out. But he knew they wouldn't get far in such a short time and Jean would need to rest after her ordeal at the hands of Frazer and the long ride she'd undertaken. He needed a plan, for himself as well as the couple in Paradise. Jesse could see himself in a cell next to Frazer if the law found out that he had warned them.

It seemed almost an eternity to Jesse before his three bunkies emerged from the saloon.

'Out with it, Jesse,' said Johnny Diamond. 'What can we do for you?'

Jesse explained what he had learned about Jean and also his intentions. The three men looked at him with open mouths.

'I knew there was something...' Johnny sought for the word, 'strange about Kelly – Jean. Who could believe she was Hay Bassett's woman and had held up a bank!'

'I'm sure she didn't do it voluntarily,' Jesse said in her defence. 'After all, she escaped from them once, only to be brought back again. I feel sorry for her.' He looked away from the men's searching eyes.

'We all know that!' Joel said. 'That's your trouble, Jesse. A woman – or even a cow – only has to look at you with big eyes and you go all mushy.'

Jesse allowed a small smile to cross his lips as he knew he had a reputation for trying to help anyone in distress, especially of the female variety.

'I'm gonna rent a fresh horse and go back up to Paradise right now,' said Jesse. 'If you can, I want you to come up with some plan to delay the sheriff from following me. I've got to get as much time between us as possible.'

'That's a tall order, Jesse,' was Jude's surprising interjection. 'We're not exactly well known for thinking up bright plans.'

Jesse gave the man a playful, light punch on his shoulder.

'Waal, for heaven's sake try your best, you hear? Try anything. Become the best darn actors the country's ever known. If anyone wants to know where I am, you've no idea.'

The men all nodded.

'We could become the best darn liars in the country, will that do?' Johnny Diamond asked with a grin.

'We could come with you?' Joel suggested.

'No. But you could accompany the sheriff. Tell him you've still got some gear in the cabin you want to fetch, and that you'd like to be helpful to him by showing him the way.' Jesse gave a short laugh. 'Who knows, you might even get a bit lost on your way up there. In fact I'd like it mighty fine if you could get the sheriff quite a bit lost.'

The men laughed and nodded in agreement. They assured him they would do their best, which Jesse had no doubt about.

He left them and made his way to the stable to give his grey a well-earned rest and fix himself up with a fresh mount. He would ride for as long as it was light, and maybe a bit longer.

The sooner he reached Paradise the happier he would be. There was no way he could sit back and allow Jean to fall into the hands of the law and be forced to serve her sentence.

The restaurant was still open when Jesse rode from the stable on a fresh horse. It had been quite a while since he had eaten, he suddenly remembered, and thought it best to get a meal before he started back to Paradise.

After the meal, Jesse set off and began thinking about Jean again. He realized that he did not know the full story of her life. For all he knew, she could have killed when she escaped from the prison wagon. If that was the case, then she would face more than just a prison sentence for the bank hold-up. She would face the hangman.

CHAPTER SEVENTEEN

Kelly and Steve arrived at the narrow track to Paradise. The wagon was still where Steve had left it and when he dismounted and looked inside, he saw that none of the provisions had been unpacked and taken to the cabin.

'Are we taking all this stuff with us, Steve?' Kelly asked him.

'Some of it. We'll leave the barrel of oil, nails and heavy stuff here, but we'll take some of the food and fill a barrel with water. We'll need some feed for the horses, too.'

Kelly gave a sigh. 'If only we dare go into Hazelworth and board a train somewhere.'

'We'd bump into the law on our way, I reckon,' was Steve's opinion.

Kelly nodded. 'I'll be sorry to leave here, Steve. If only those three from the insurance company hadn't turned up.'

'Yeah,' Steve growled, 'that Frazer in particular. I shoulda killed him!'

Kelly shook her head. 'I would have agreed with you a while back, but it's best the law deals with him. He's only got to be hung once.'

'Sure,' Steve agreed, 'but I'd like them to do it real slow.'

Steve unpacked some of the stuff they would not need to take with them and left it on the wide part of the track.

'We'll collect Doc Reynolds' legacy, then we must be off again,' Steve told her. He noticed the sad expression on her face, and also the fact that she looked very tired. He knew she ought to rest after what she had

153

been through, in addition to the long ride. He worried that she might lose the baby.

'I've just gotta take a bath, Steve,' she told him. 'That animal has made me feel dirty.'

Steve hesitated. He knew how she was feeling, but he also knew they did not have a lot of time before the law came upon them. Kelly read his thoughts.

'Making Frazer walk back to Hazelworth should give us a bit of time. I have a feeling Jesse knew why I wanted him to walk bare-footed.'

'Jesse.'

Kelly looked at him sharply. His face was grim and she tried to read his thoughts.

'He was good to me, Steve,' she informed him.

'Yeah,' he said. 'How good, Kelly?'

Kelly frowned. 'What are you getting at?'

'That man is in love with you and you know it. Just how friendly did you two become?' he demanded to know.

'Steve!' Kelly exclaimed. 'You're being stupid! He protected me. He was like a father to me, one I've never had.'

Steve did not answer but urged his horse on over the narrow track.

Kelly felt hurt and bewildered. How could he think things like that? That she could possibly fall in love with another man after all she and Steve had been through to be together. She tried to blink away the tears, but they came anyway.

Steve dismounted outside the cabin and lifted her down from the saddle. He looked down at her face and noticed the tears. The next second she found herself in his arms and he held her close.

'I'm so sorry,' he whispered. 'You're right, I am stupid. I should be grateful to the man for taking care of you. I guess he was as angry as I was that he couldn't stop Frazer from doing what he did to you. I love you, Kelly, and I get jealous when another man looks at you the way Jesse did.'

Kelly nodded and preceded him into the cabin.

'I'll get the stove going,' she said. 'Bring that tin bath inside, will you? And fill the big pan with water for the stove.'

Kelly got the stove to light and she began to feel so tired. She crossed over to the bed intending to shut her eyes for five minutes or so, but she fell asleep completely, for half an hour in fact, by which time the water was ready for her bath.

Steve poured out the water for her and left the cabin to see to the horses. He realized they would need a rest and a good feed before they could use them again. He did not know how far they would need to go, but it would be a good idea to get out of the county, and the sooner the better. He wondered if the sheriff had found out that there was a Kelly and Steve living in the cabin. The cowboys were bound to let drop what their names were.

Kelly was about to step out of the bath when Steve returned from seeing to the horses. He caught his breath at the sight of her. She was so beautiful. He stood in the doorway and was in complete awe of her, her long flame-coloured hair surrounding her white shoulders and her lithe form silhouetted in the light from the window and open cabin door.

She turned as he entered and Steve averted his eyes so as not to embarrass her with his stare.

'You can lift me out if you like, Steve,' she smiled.

Steve picked up a towel on the chair near the tin bath, wrapped it around her body and lifted her from the water.

It felt wonderful being held by the man she loved. He held her so tightly that she could hardly breathe and his kisses almost suffocated her.

'No one will take you away from me, Kelly, no one!' he declared.

They ate a meal and cleared away. Kelly looked around the cabin and in her mind's eye she saw the faces of the Bassett gang. She had still not grown used to their not being around. Kelly had believed that she was no longer an outlaw and that her life was now settled with Steve, but she realized with sadness that it could never be settled here in Paradise. She had become an outlaw once again and had made Steve one also by his being with her.

Steve lay on his back under the table and pushed a compartment to one side. He produced the paper parcel of bank-notes which Doc Reynolds had given to Kelly when she and Jim Tobin came to the town where the doctor had settled. The more Steve thought about it, the more he realized that this money was also from the proceeds of bank robberies, and not the doctor's life savings as he had said. He must have known where the outlaws had hidden their loot and dug it up after the trials of those who used Larkinton as a hideout from the law.

Kelly picked up the coffee pot and a skillet and was about to gather up their pillows from the bed.

'You can't carry all that lot.' Steve smiled. 'I'll take the pillows and some blankets. We may have to sleep in the wagon or under it for a few nights.'

He looked around for the last time. 'Are you ready?' he asked her.

She nodded. 'Let's go.'

They carried what belongings they wanted to take with them over the track to the wagon and returned for the horses, riding them over the track for the very last time.

Steve hitched them up to the wagon and held the bridle of one of them as he turned the wagon around in the direction of Larkinton, two miles on.

He looked at her as she sat by his side. She still looked tired and strained.

'Look on this as a new beginning, Kelly,' he said. 'There are too many memories in Paradise. There would always be something there that would come between us – Hay, Jim...'

She nodded. 'You're right, Steve. A new beginning.'

Joel, Johnny and Jude enjoyed the rest of the evening. That was until Joel accidentally knocked into someone carrying a full glass of beer and spilt some of it.

'Sorry, mister,' Joel apologized at once.

It might have ended there peacefully had the man carrying the drink not had a few too many already. He took offence at Joel's clumsiness and wanted to make something out of it.

'You can buy me another one for that!' the man said, almost falling over with intoxication.

'It don't warrant that, mister!' Joel declared. 'You hardly spilt a drop.'

'I'll have another one on you or you can go for your gun,' said the drunk, slurring his words.

Joel turned to ignore the man, but as his back was turned he heard the sound of the hammer being cocked on the man's gun.

There had to be a split-second decision. The man's gun was all ready to fire, Joel's was still in its holster. Joel drew his gun and spun on his heel to face the drunkard. He cocked the hammer of his own weapon and pulled the trigger at the same time as the drunkard pulled his. Joel's bullet went into the man's stomach and the drunkard's went into Joel's shoulder. Both fell to the floor. Only Joel got up, holding his hand to the bloody wound.

'You all saw that!' Joel looked around him at the onlookers. 'He drew on me first, and I had my back to him!'

Heads nodded all round him. 'You weren't to blame, mister!' someone called across the room. 'He was asking for it.'

A man came pushing forward, a gun in his hand. He was wearing a star on his vest.

'Hand over your gun, mister!' the lawman demanded.

'It weren't his fault, Pete!' someone in the room called out. 'He tried to avoid a fight but Barney insisted.'

'I don't care a damn whose fault it was,' the deputy said, taking Joel's gun. 'Go on, feller, walk ahead of me – to the sheriff's office.'

'I think he's still alive,' said Joel as he passed by the prone body of Barney. He was still breathing, but blood oozed from the man's stomach.

'Fer the moment,' the deputy replied, 'but not fer much longer, I reckon. Now walk ahead of me – pronto!'

Johnny and Jude followed behind the deputy sheriff. There was no way they were going to leave their bunkie in the hands of the law, especially not while he was injured.

'Tom, go and fetch the doctor quick!' the

deputy asked of one of the men near the bar. 'And after he's seen to Barney, send him over to the jail.'

'Sure thing, Pete.' Tom scurried off.

'The end of a perfect evening!' Johnny Diamond mumbled, and the friends trooped out of the saloon behind the deputy.

CHAPTER EIGHTEEN

An hour later, Doctor Peters entered the sheriff's office carrying his black bag.

'In here, Doc,' Sheriff Todd told him. He picked up the keys to the cells and led the way through a door at the back of the office.

Joel was sitting on a bunk. His shoulder had been bandaged in a fashion to try to stop the bleeding. There was a hole in his back where the bullet had obviously passed through his shoulder and out the other side. This at least would save the doctor having to probe for it.

'You took your time, didn't you?' Joel growled.

'Shut your mouth!' the deputy ordered. 'Your wound weren't so bad as Barney's.'

He turned to the doctor. 'How *is* Barney, Doc?'

'His wound was fatal, I'm afraid. He died just before I got there.'

The cell door was unlocked and the doctor went in.

'Now let's have a look at you, he said. 'You cowboys!' He shook his head. 'There's always trouble when cowboys come into town.'

'Just hold on there, Doc!' Johnny Diamond exploded. 'We weren't making no trouble. This Barney feller was intent on picking a fight. He even pulled his gun on Joel when he turned his back on him. What was he supposed to do – just let himself get plugged?'

Sheriff Todd had been watching the men's faces and he felt sure they were telling the truth. He knew for a fact that Barney Noble was constantly drunk, but he also knew that cowboys were in the habit of getting drunk and making trouble. But these men before him seemed sober enough.

'Hold the fort, Pete!' Todd told his deputy. 'I'm going to the saloon for some answers.'

The sheriff left his office and made his way to the saloon. Barney's body had been removed and some sawdust had been sprinkled over the blood near the bar.

''Evenin', Ray,' he said to the barkeep.

'You've had a bit of trouble in here tonight, I hear?'

Ray continued polishing glasses as he answered:

'Yeah, Sheriff. You've come to get the lowdown, I reckon?'

'What happened? Who started it?' Todd wanted to know.

Ray related the events and confirmed what the sheriff had already been told.

'Thanks, Ray. I guess I'll have to let the cowboy go.'

Ray nodded and continued polishing the glasses.

Back at his office the sheriff confronted Johnny and Jude, who were awaiting his return.

'Seems like it was self-defence,' Todd told the two. 'I'll let him out in the morning. He may as well stay where he is until then. Then he can hand over five dollars for his board for the night.'

The two cowboys considered arguing with this decision, but on looking at the sheriff's stern face, they decided against it and left. Joel would do no harm where he was and no harm was likely to come to him.

Todd followed the two outside. He was going home for the night, leaving his deputy in charge.

'You'll be going up to Paradise tomorrow, won't you, Sheriff?' Johnny Diamond asked him.

'You must've been talking to that other cowboy who came in here with a feller named Franks and towing another on a bit of rope by his neck, called Frazer.'

'Yeah, he's our bunkie. Jesse, us two and Joel in the jail were all there when Frazer shot Mr Richards down in cold blood and took off with the loot and a girl as hostage so we wouldn't follow. I hear you're going up to Paradise to bring in the girl and her feller?'

Todd nodded. 'I'll need to gather one or two men to accompany me. I'm going home for a sleep so we'll make a fresh start in the morning.'

Johnny smiled at the man in a friendly fashion.

'We've got to go back up there, Sheriff, to fetch the rest of our gear we left behind when we followed Jesse a bit later on.'

'Accompanied by a man called Steve Culley,' Todd added.

Johnny shrugged. 'His name was Steve. I don't know his other name.'

'Well I can assure you that it is Culley,'

said Todd. 'And the girl's name is Kelly.'

'I don't know about that, Sheriff,' Jude interjected. 'She said her name was Jean, and that's what we called her.'

'Her name is Kelly,' Todd said firmly. 'That Frazer feller who I've got locked up in the jail told me so.'

Johnny's face clouded with anger. 'And you'd rather believe a murderer, would you, Sheriff?'

'I've been told her hair's the same colour as the Kelly I knew. Red.' Todd moved off, eager to get home and get some sleep. Johnny and Jude hurried after him.

'We'll come with you in the morning, Sheriff. Have you been up to Paradise before?' asked Johnny.

'No. Marshal Dalton dealt with it all before. It'll be easy enough to find, I guess.'

'We'll show you the way,' Jude offered. 'It's easy to miss if you're not careful.'

'OK.' Todd nodded. 'I'll see you boys at eight o'clock sharp outside my office tomorrow.'

Jude and Johnny exchanged conspiratorial smiles and moved off to the hotel to get a room for the night.

Pete Thomas was in charge of the jail for the

night. He liked being in charge as it gave him a sense of importance and nothing much ever happened anyway, so he could put his feet up on the desk and have a snooze.

Before this happened, however, Andy Crawford would come to the office with the deputy's supper and a meal for any prisoners in the jail.

'Here's your supper, Pete,' he said, plonking the plate down in front of the deputy, spilling some of the gravy on to some papers on the desk.

'Careful with that!' Pete growled. 'We've got two in there tonight,' he jerked his thumb at the door at the end of the office, 'so you'll have to go back to the restaurant for them.'

'OK, Pete.' Andy nodded and left the deputy to enjoy his supper.

By the time Andy returned, Pete had finished his supper. He took the two meals into the jail. He put them down on a side table just inside the door while he unlocked Joel's cell first and put the plate on the ledge inside. He ducked out of the cell quickly before Joel stood up, and relocked the cell door.

He moved down to Frazer's cell and unlocked it. As he was putting the meal down on the ledge, Frazer called him over.

166

'I've got something important to tell you, Deputy. I don't want *him* hearing.'

Pete Thomas walked over to the man who was lying on his bunk. Frazer sat up and moved his head forward as if to whisper in the deputy's ear.

The next second the deputy was twisted around by his arms and Frazer pulled one of the legs from the bunk, which he had obviously removed before and had been propped back in position so it would not be noticed. The deputy received a mighty crack on the back of his head. He lay still on the cell floor. Frazer took the deputy's gun, picked up his keys and locked the lawman inside the cell.

'You won't get far, Frazer!' Joel shouted after the fleeing figure.

'Wanna bet?' Frazer called after him, locking the door to the cells and depositing the keys in the potbellied stove.

Frazer inched his way around the sheriff's office door and looked up and down the street. There were several horses tied up outside the saloon and Frazer walked slowly along the sidewalk. To run would only draw attention to himself.

He picked out a sturdy-looking bay and mounted up, riding at a leisurely pace until he got to the other end of town. Then he kicked the horse in its flanks and rode off into the night – in the direction of Paradise.

It was an hour before sundown when Jesse reached Larkinton. He had ridden his mount far harder than he knew he ought to have done, but there would be time for the animal to rest once he had reached Paradise.

After riding through the burnt-out town and another two miles to the narrow track, Jesse felt the strong desire to see Jean's sweet face once more before she and Steve had to leave Paradise for ever.

He reached the other side and passed between the two boulders. The cabin came into view, but there was no smoke coming from the chimney. There had been no wagon on the other side of the track, Jesse remembered. And there were no horses in the corral.

He ran towards the cabin and up the two steps leading to the door. He flung it open, knowing full well that there was no one inside.

There was not much light inside but he could see well enough that he was right. The pair had already fled.

Jesse walked across to the stove and put his hand close to the metal. There was no heat coming from it so he put his hand fully on it. It was cold. They had obviously left quite a while ago. He looked around the cabin. The coffee pot was gone, so was the skillet. The pillows and blankets were missing from the bed and the few clothes that had been in the cupboard were no longer there.

Jesse sat down on the bed and a long sigh escaped him. She was gone – and he missed her already.

After a while a smile came to his weather-beaten, kindly face. It was well she had gone, for the more distance she put between her and the law, the better it would be for her. He realized that he would rather never see her again and she be safe, than see her again and she be taken in by the law and maybe given a far harder sentence than the ten years she had failed to serve.

'Goodbye, my sweet Jean. Stay safe, my love,' he whispered to the empty cabin.

Jesse stood up, walked across to the window and looked out. He knew he would remember this scene for as long as he lived.

There were things to do. He had to take care of the horse before nightfall and then he would take care of himself. A good meal and a good sleep. That was what was required.

CHAPTER NINETEEN

The deputy lay still. He had remained that way for about ten minutes, Joel reckoned, and not a sound had come from him. He wondered if he were dead. At least he could not be accused of his murder, for he was still locked up in his cell.

Joel began banging on the bars of his cell with his metal cup. He was not sure if any sound would penetrate through the sheriff's office on the other side of the locked door into the open street. What would make anyone outside take any notice of his attempts to attract attention? he wondered. He suddenly had an idea.

'Fire! Fire! Fire!' he yelled at the top of his voice and followed it with more banging on his cell bars.

There was no response for several minutes, then after what seemed an eternity, someone came to the door leading to the cells.

'What's going on in there?' came a man's voice. 'I can't smell any smoke.'

'You've gotta get help!' Joel yelled. 'A

prisoner called Frazer has knocked out the deputy and locked him in a cell and escaped. I think he's pretty bad. He's been out cold for quite a while now. Hurry it up!'

There was silence for a moment, then the man on the other side of the door replied, 'OK, but this had better not be a trick.'

Joel waited impatiently. If he was going to be incarcerated for the night, he would have preferred to have been left in peace so he could get some sleep to prevent him from feeling the pain in his shoulder. It had bled a bit since the doctor had attended to it and Joel began to wonder just how bad the wound was. Luckily it was his left shoulder, otherwise it might have made him lose the use of his right hand.

He began to start thinking about Jesse and whether he had reached Paradise by now. The boys had not known the girl for long, but he knew they were all concerned about her safety. He hoped Jesse could warn them in time so they could get a good start away from the Bassett gang's former hideout. Joel had planned to go with his two bunkies in the morning on the pretext of showing the sheriff the way there, leading him on a roundabout route to give Jean and Steve more time to get away, but he wondered if he would be up to the journey so soon after receiving the bullet wound.

Joel was becoming more impatient by the minute. Where was that man he'd spoken to on the other side of the door? Why hadn't he returned with help?

At last he heard voices.

'Where are the keys?' a voice called out.

'Frazer locked the door and left with them. I guess you'll have to break the door down. You'll have to find a locksmith or a stick of dynamite for the cell doors.'

There were mumblings on the other side of the door and Joel heard the words: '...using it as an excuse to make a getaway...'

Three burly figures put their shoulders to the door and after three attempts the door burst open.

'Get some light in here!' one of them said.

A lamp was produced and in the dim light the men could see the deputy lying on the floor in one cell and Joel, with a bandaged shoulder in another.

'How long ago did this happen?' one of the men asked Joel.

'It seems a pretty long time to me,' Joel replied. 'Someone had better get these cell doors open pretty quick so the doctor can check on Pete here.'

'I'll wake Tom up,' said a man in a black frock-coat and a black string tie.

Joel thought he recognized the man from the night before. He had spoken up for him after the shooting. He recalled that he had been in a serious poker-game in the far corner.

'Who's Tom?' Joel asked.

'The blacksmith. He'll get the doors open.'

'Has anyone sent for the doctor?' Joel asked.

'Yeah, he'll be here soon,' another of the men said.

Just then a short man with a balding head rushed into the sheriff's office.

'Someone stole my horse!' he panted. 'Where's the sheriff?'

'At home in bed,' the gambler replied. 'Come back in the morning.'

'I wouldn't be one bit surprised if Frazer rode off on it,' Joel put forward.

'He won't get very far,' the erstwhile owner of the horse informed the gathered men. 'It lost a shoe on my way into town. I was gonna take it to the blacksmith in the morning.'

Joel gave a short, mirthless laugh. 'That'll teach him to pick the wrong horse!' Joel smiled to himself as he pictured Frazer out on the open plains without a mount. He wondered if anyone had seen him leave town, and in which direction.

After about half an hour had elapsed, Sheriff Daniel Todd, the doctor and the blacksmith arrived. The blacksmith's services were called on first and the big, broad-shouldered man soon had the cell containing the deputy open. The doctor then went inside and examined Pete.

The MD gave a sigh and shook his head.

'Dead,' he pronounced. 'He's cold, so he must have died a while ago.' He looked through the bars at Joel and could see some blood on his bandage.

'Open this cell too, Tom,' he asked the blacksmith. 'I'll take a look at the cowboy again while I'm here. And you can let him out now,' he turned to face the others. 'He was going to be released in the morning anyway.'

Joel sat on the bunk ready for the doctor to enter the cell.

'If it's all the same to you, Doc, I'll stay put till morning. I may as well make use of the bunk. I'll be charged for the privilege anyhow.'

The doctor smiled. Although Joel had

killed Barney, he was well aware that there was no real harm in the man and that it had been Barney's own fault.

Some soothing ointment was applied to the wound and it was rebandaged.

'It's not too bad,' the doctor pronounced. 'You'll be able to ride in the morning. I know you were going with your friends and the sheriff up to Paradise.'

Joel nodded. 'Thanks, Doc.'

Sheriff Todd arrived at his office much sooner than he had intended. Morning had been his original choice. Joel could see the man was irritated at being disturbed, but his face changed noticeably when he heard that his deputy was dead.

'That bastard Frazer!' he growled. 'I'll get him if it's the last thing I ever do!'

'You'd better find out which way he headed first,' was Joel's opinion.

'I'm perfectly aware of that fact!' Todd spat.

A small, bespectacled man still wearing a nightshirt tucked inside his trousers, ran into the office then.

'Sheriff!' he yelled unnecessarily as no one in the room was deaf, 'I saw a feller riding outa town on Ted Rimmer's bay. I thought it was Ted at first but when he reached the end of town, he rode far too fast fer him!'

Everyone knew where Cornelius Pratt lived, which was opposite the rail station, so it was obvious that Frazer was heading west.

'Thanks, Corny.' Todd patted the small man on the shoulder. 'You've saved me a lot of time going round asking people if they'd seen which way he went.'

Corny beamed with pride that he had been of some help. At least it was some consolation for not being tucked up in his warm bed, which he had been about to get into when he saw the fleeing figure on Ted Rimmer's horse from his bedroom window.

Todd looked thoughtful for a minute. He was now without a deputy and he himself would have to go after not only Kelly and Steve up in Paradise, but now Frazer. The town would be without any law while he was gone. He caught sight of Joel, still sitting on the bunk in the cell. He stood at the open cell door and hesitated before he spoke to him.

'You're well enough to ride, the doctor said.'

'So I've been told,' replied Joel.

'You didn't ought to tire yourself too soon,' came the sheriff's unexpected words. It sounded as if the lawman was concerned for Joel's state of health. 'I'm wondering...' he hesitated, shifting his feet a little uneasily, 'I was wondering if you'd do me a mighty big favour.'

Joel frowned. 'And what's that, Sheriff?'

'I need a deputy right now. At least until I get back to town with the criminals. I don't think you're quite ready to be riding around at the moment. If you stay in town, it will give your shoulder chance to heal.'

Joel gave a surprised smile. 'You mean you're asking me to become a deputy sheriff?' he asked.

The sheriff nodded. 'I'd be much obliged.'

Joel thought the matter over for a few seconds before replying:

'How come you think I'm deputy material when I've been locked up for the night?' he asked.

'Needs must. You've killed, but you're no killer. It won't be for long – I hope,' the sheriff concluded.

Joel thought it over again, then nodded his agreement.

'OK, just as long as we don't suddenly get an influx of rowdy cowboys shootin' up the town. Those darn cowboys are a real menace!'

The twinkle in Joel's eye at the irony of the

situation was not lost on the sheriff.

'Thanks,' said the lawman, and promptly pinned a star on Joel's vest pocket. 'Raise your right hand!'

Joel did so.

'Repeat after me: I solemnly swear to uphold the law of this county.'

Joel repeated the words. 'Now, can I get back to sleep till morning?' he asked.

CHAPTER TWENTY

With Frazer to catch besides bringing in Kelly and Steve, Sheriff Todd was forced to deputize more men to join the posse. He rounded up half a dozen men besides Johnny and Jude. He wrote out a telegraph message to the next town west of Hazelworth for the law to look out for all three fugitives before the posse set off.

When the sheriff and posse had left, Joel read through the message before taking it over to the telegraph office.

'Hm,' he mumbled to himself. 'There are far too many words here. I'll strike a few off to save the county some money.' With a smile on his face he crossed off all reference to Kelly and Steve, but left the description of Frazer on the message.

Johnny and Jude were unaware of the happenings of the night before and things were a bit different now. They knew they could delay the sheriff if he had come alone, or with another couple of men, but now the posse consisted of six more riders. It would be more difficult to send the men on a wild-goose chase around the country, and in any case Frazer had to be caught – fast.

Johnny's mind was ticking over and an idea came to him.

'As we're trailing two lots of criminals, mebbe we ought to split up. Half of us go up to Paradise for the girl and Steve Culley and the other half ride on after Frazer?' Johnny suggested to the sheriff.

'I guess it would save some time,' Todd replied. 'I'll take three men and go after Frazer and you two cowboys take another three and go up to Paradise.'

'What do we do with them when we find them, Sheriff?' Jude asked worriedly. 'We can hardly just shoot them.'

'Arrest them if you can, but if they resist, then you'll have to shoot them. Disarm them first if you're able to. And don't be fooled by the girl's sweet face. She can shoot as well as any man.'

Before the posse arrived at the entrance to the box canyon they could see a bay horse in the distance. There was no sign of Frazer.

'What do you make of that?' one of the posse remarked.

'Frazer's obviously now on foot,' said Todd. 'He got quite a way on a horse with one shoe missing. I guess he rode it to its limit.'

'Larkinton can't be too far off,' said Johnny. 'It's my bet he'll make for there, and Paradise.'

The posse all looked at Johnny and agreed.

'I reckon we don't need to split up now,' said Todd. 'Come on, boys – before Mr Frazer and the last of the Bassett gang shoot it out.'

'What if they do?' A posse member gave a short laugh. 'It'll save us having to do it.'

Johnny and Jude were of the opposite opinion. And where did Jesse stand in all this? they wondered.

It was around mid-morning when Jesse sat down to a meal he had prepared for himself. It seemed strange eating alone after such a long time. The more hours that passed before the law arrived in Paradise, then the more time Jean and Steve had to get away.

A thought suddenly occurred to him. The sheriff would no doubt have telegraphed ahead to the next town to look out for the couple. If that was the case, then all those hours would have been wasted and they would be riding into a reception committee. Why had he not thought about this before? he wondered. Jesse realized then that there was nothing more he could do. He decided to go for a walk down by the pool and wait until the law arrived.

Darkness fell before the posse had reached Larkinton and they were forced to rest for the night. Frazer was midway between Larkinton and Paradise and sat down with his back against a rock until it was light enough to see to cross the narrow track. He had walked for miles and his feet were sore. They had not fully recovered from his long forced march in bare feet and naked to Hazelworth. He cursed the girl for humiliating him and he intended making her pay. If he met up again with Jesse, he would kill the man.

At first light Frazer set off along the narrow track. The rest had helped some, but his feet still hurt. His stomach growled too.

He would force the girl to cook him a meal when he got to the cabin.

Frazer checked the gun he had taken from the deputy and, satisfied that the chamber was full, pushed it back into the belt of his pants. When he reached the two boulders he could see smoke coming from the chimney in the cabin. He made his way along by the corral out of sight of the cabin window.

As he passed the corral he noticed there was only one horse in there. He did not recognize it. Why were there not two, or even three? he wondered.

He made his way silently to the door and gave it a slight push with the barrel of his gun. He stood in the doorway as his eyes slowly became accustomed to the gloom inside. There was no one there.

Jesse buckled the belt to his pants as he came through the door of the privy. He saw a movement at the cabin door and realized that someone had gone inside. His hand instinctively went to his gun and he drew it. He knew he would be in line with the door and window and he dodged behind the privy so he could make his way to the corral with a better chance of not being seen. But he had been. A bullet flew past his right ear and he quickened to a run.

Jesse knew the man inside stood a better chance, as the cabin was sturdily built and the door could be bolted, preventing access. But Jesse also knew that the man would get pretty thirsty after a while for there was no water inside the cabin and the coffeepot was empty. On the other hand, the man inside the cabin had food, whereas Jesse had none. But Jesse knew a man could go longer without food than water. In any event, the posse should arrive pretty soon, he reckoned.

Jesse pressed himself against the side of the cabin and waited. He was a patient man and was prepared to wait for as long as it took.

After a while Jesse peered cautiously around the side of the cabin, just as the man inside poked his head around the doorway. The man was Frazer!

Jesse dodged back and sucked in his breath. What in heaven's name was *he* doing here? What had happened back at the jail? Whom had he killed to escape?

Frazer's heartbeats were faster now. The man he wanted to meet was here and there was no one around to watch the forthcoming showdown.

'Come on out, Frazer!' Jesse shouted. 'You can't stay in there for ever.'

'Go to hell, Jesse!' came the reply.

'I'd rather not, not just yet anyhow. Feeling thirsty yet?' he goaded.

There was no answer for a moment or two, then Frazer asked:

'Where's the girl, and her man?'

'Gone,' Jesse answered.

'The law will get them!' Frazer promised.

'And you, Frazer. There can be no doubt about that.'

There was silence again and Jesse wondered what the man could be plotting. He was also wondering how far away the law was at that moment and how soon help would arrive.

At least Jesse knew that he was between Frazer and the only horse. He was sure the horse would be Frazer's next objective.

Time passed. Now the sun was directly above and by this, and the fact that Jesse's stomach was beginning to growl, he knew it must be midday.

'Are you getting hungry, Jesse?' Frazer shouted out.

'Just a bit,' Jesse replied. 'What about you – are you feeling thirsty?'

Jesse smiled to himself when Frazer did not reply. He was feeling thirsty himself by now and made his way via the corral to the stream. No bullet followed him so he reckoned he'd made it without being noticed. He lay on his stomach and cupped his hands into the water. It tasted good. He remained where he was for the moment. A boulder sheltered him from view of the cabin and he was able to watch the door from his position.

Then he noticed Frazer inching himself away from the door, keeping his back to the wall as he made his way to the corner of the cabin where Jesse had been previously. Jesse also realized that he could be making his way to the horse as well.

Just as Frazer reached the corner and peered around it, Jesse came out of his hideout behind the boulder and started forward towards his adversary.

'I'm over here, Frazer!' he called. As the man spun round Jesse's gun barked. Frazer's arms seemed to rise into the air as he crumpled to the ground, his gun falling from his hand.

Jesse walked slowly up to the man. When he reached him he pushed his body over on to his back with his foot. The bullet had entered his heart and Frazer was obviously dead. It gave Jesse no pleasure that he had killed the man, but he was glad it was all over. He left Frazer where he lay and went into the cabin for a pail to fill up so he could get himself a cup of coffee.

An hour or two later Jesse heard horses outside the cabin. He went to the door and recognized the sheriff, Johnny and Jude and six other men. But there was no Joel with them.

Todd dismounted first and bent down to examine Frazer's dead body.

'That's one out of the way. Where's Kelly and Steve?' he asked Jesse.

'I found them...' there was a long pause, 'gone.' Jesse lowered his eyes to the ground and the men could sense the sadness in them.

Todd frowned deeply. He supposed Jesse meant that the two had already left, but by the way he'd said it, 'gone' could have meant they were both dead, probably killed by Frazer, who'd had a mighty big axe to grind.

'I'd like to take a look around,' Todd said. 'What's down there in the valley?'

'Not much,' Jesse answered. 'A pool. A forest. Mountains.'

'I'd like to look anyway,' said Todd. He started off towards the valley. Everyone followed him.

'Where's Joel?' Jesse asked of his two

bunkies. 'You didn't leave him in bed with that saloon girl, did you?'

They laughed and shook their heads.

'You'll never believe this, Jesse,' said Jude, 'but Joel's Hazelworth's new deputy sheriff. He's taking care of the town right now while the sheriff's up here. Frazer killed the other deputy and made his escape. If the horse he stole hadn't lost a shoe, he would have probably kept riding and not called in up here. I'll tell you the rest later.'

They reached the pool. Todd looked around him.

He was looking at the two graves.

'These graves are freshly dug!' he exclaimed. 'Who's in them?'

Jesse gave Johnny a light kick on his ankle to stop him from talking.

When there was no reply, Todd looked directly at Jesse.

'Did you dig these graves?' he asked him.

Jesse nodded, but did not forward any other information. He had no intention of telling the lawman that they had dug the graves up to find the outlaws' loot. He could tell Todd was putting two and two together and coming up with five.

'Why didn't you leave the bodies for the law to take care of? I need to identify them.'

'I couldn't bear to see her body being paraded around town, like some circus freak. If anyone was gonna bury her, it had to be me – right here where she lived.'

Todd considered insisting that Jesse or one of the other men dig up the graves for his inspection, but on seeing Jesse's brilliantly acted crestfallen face, he decided against it. It was obvious that the girl had come to mean something to Jesse while they had lived together over the last few days, and he couldn't put the man through any more grief.

'What about the man Richards' body. I believe it's in the barn?' Todd asked.

'That's right, Sheriff. We didn't know the man right well, so we didn't bury him,' said Johnny. 'He might be going off a bit by now.'

Todd wrinkled his nose slightly at the thought of the now decomposing body.

'What's happening now, Jesse?' Jude asked as they all walked back to the cabin.

'Waal, it sounds as if Joel's got himself a steady job – fer a while, anyhow.' Jesse grinned. 'It's up to you. We could stay here, or move on and look for work to tide us through the winter.'

'Ain't you fergettin' something, Jesse?' Johnny said.

Jesse looked at him, a frown on his face.

'We've got a bit of money behind us now. We could put it together and buy ourselves a small spread of our own. We could even go in for horses, you bein' an expert in that department.'

Jesse smiled broadly. 'We could at that!' he enthused.

Sheriff Todd stopped suddenly.

'Just a minute! If Kelly and Steve are buried in those graves, just where the hell are their horses?' Todd demanded.

This jolted Jesse for the moment and he thought fast.

'They're probably around somewhere. They were grazing near the forest. Have we got to go round looking for them?'

Todd thought for a moment, then decided he couldn't spare the time. They weren't his horses anyway and they would be happy where they were.

Jesse, Johnny and Jude decided to go back to Hazelworth with the posse to see whether Joel wanted to be a lawman or a landowner. Knowing Joel as they did, he had probably already spent most of the money he'd received as a reward for finding the loot.

On the way back to Hazelworth, Jesse's mind went to Jean, as he still thought of her.

He wondered how she and Steve were faring.

He would have been glad to know that all was well with the couple. Although Kelly didn't know it, the law considered her dead – for the second time in her life – and no one would be looking for them. America was a big country. Big enough to get lost in.

The publishers hope that this book has given you enjoyable reading. Large Print Books are especially designed to be as easy to see and hold as possible. If you wish a complete list of our books please ask at your local library or write directly to:

Dales Large Print Books
Magna House, Long Preston,
Skipton, North Yorkshire.
BD23 4ND

This Large Print Book, for people
who cannot read normal print,
is published under the auspices of

THE ULVERSCROFT FOUNDATION

... we hope you have enjoyed this book.
Please think for a moment about those
who have worse eyesight than you ...
and are unable to even read or enjoy
Large Print without great difficulty.

You can help them by sending a
donation, large or small, to:

**The Ulverscroft Foundation,
1, The Green, Bradgate Road,
Anstey, Leicestershire, LE7 7FU,
England.**
or request a copy of our brochure for
more details.

The Foundation will use all donations
to assist those people who are visually
impaired and need special attention
with medical research, diagnosis
and treatment.

Thank you very much for your help.